PENNY JORDAN

Law of Attraction

D0057272

Harlequin Books

TORONTO • NEW YORK • LONDON
AMSTERDAM • PARIS • SYDNEY • HAMBURG
STOCKHOLM • ATHENS • TOKYO • MILAN
MADRID • WARSAW • BUDAPEST • AUCKLAND

ISBN 0-373-11705-1

LAW OF ATTRACTION

CHAPTER ONE

CHARLOTTE paused outside the block of offices, studying the plaque which read 'Jefferson & Horwich, Solicitors'.

Her knees were trembling slightly and the skirt of her dark blue wool suit, which if anything had seemed rather prim in London, suddenly felt uncomfortably short.

She tugged at it a little self-consciously as she glanced around the busy market square.

It was only just gone eight in the morning, but it was market day and the stallholders were already hard at work preparing for their day's trading.

Perhaps she ought to have bought herself a new suit, something more suitable for a very junior, albeit qualified solicitor, just starting work in a new practice, but the trouble was that new clothes were a luxury she simply could not afford at the moment.

'Jefferson & Horwich'. She read the name again.

Well, Richard Horwich she had already met. He had interviewed her for the job. A comfortable middle-aged family man who epitomised everyone's mental image of a solicitor with a country practice.

But as for the Jefferson...

Charlotte took a deep breath.

Face it, she told herself bitterly. You would rather be working for almost anyone than Daniel Jefferson. The new golden hope of the legal profession, the man who had single-handedly—well, almost, if you excluded the odd barrister or so, and the usual full complement of legal staff—championed the cause of the downtrodden, in this case the victims of the negligent and callous refusal of a large drugs company to accept that the side-effects of their drug had caused detrimental physical symptoms in some of those people prescribed it, never mind doing anything about it, and had won for them not only recognition of the drugs company's negligence, but also one of the largest sums in compensation ever awarded by a British court.

As she stood staring at the polished brass nameplate on the front of the elegant Georgian building she couldn't help contrasting *her* circumstances with those of Daniel Jefferson.

She too was a qualified solicitor. She too had once had her own premises with her name alongside the door, and she too had once championed the cause of those who sometimes seemed most to need legal advice and who nearly always could least afford it. But there the resemblance between them ended.

Where Daniel Jefferson was successful, fêted, inundated no doubt with people wanting him to act for them, especially since the Vitalle case had made the headlines, *she* was now forced to seek work as an employee... forced to start again right at the foot of the ladder, her home, her business and even her fiancé gone, swallowed up by the recession which was slowly strangling and destroying so many businesses.

Perhaps she ought, as her parents and her friends kept telling her, to feel grateful that she had been able to get another job with such relative ease instead of still being so full of anger and resentment about all that she had lost.

But she *was* angry and she was resentful. She had worked so hard. First just when she was studying, and then in her first job as the only female newly qualified solicitor in the large London practice where she had been lucky enough to be employed.

She had even learned to bite on her tongue and not to retaliate when the men she worked with tried to demote and degrade her, giving her the dullest and most routine jobs, and even on one infuriating occasion actually asking her to make coffee for the rest of them. Yes, she had worked hard then, and always with one goal in mind. Her own practice... and before she was thirty.

She had been over the moon when by what had seemed to be the most amazingly fortuitous stroke of good luck she and Bevan, her fiancé, had happened to come across a small local single-partner practice for sale.

It had been just about the time that people were moving out of London in swarms, extolling the virtues of country living, and, as Bevan had told her, she would have been a fool not to have jumped on the bandwagon.

She had bought the practice with a mortgage the size of which had made her wince. And she had also bought herself a small elegant town house several streets away.

After all, as she and Bevan had agreed, once they were married the town house would be large enough for them both, and then later they could sell it at a decent profit and buy something larger.

Their part of the world was an up-and-coming area with property prices going through the roof, as Charlotte had discovered when she was gazumped both on the house and on the business. Fortunately she had been able to borrow enough to outbid the would-be gazumpers, but that had left her with no cash at all and a large overdraft as well as her huge mortgage.

She *had* been a little afraid then, but Bevan had laughed at her. What was wrong with her? he had demanded. She was only taking the same kind of risk that men had to take all the time. 'What is it with you women?' he had challenged her. 'You want equality and then when you get it...'

He had shrugged without finishing his sentence, but she had known what he was implying.

Bevan was inclined to be irritable and quick to make judgements. He lived a very high-powered existence as a dealer working in the City.

Charlotte had met him through a colleague and at first she had been a little put off by his manner, but he had pursued her so determinedly that she had not been able to help being flattered.

Their engagement was an unofficial, casual arrangement, more a declaration of an intent to marry once they had both achieved a certain status in their lifestyles than a formal betrothal.

Charlotte knew that her parents, especially her mother, were a little perplexed with this arrangement. An engagement, to her mother, meant a diamond ring and a date fixed for the wedding.

Charlotte had had neither the ring nor the date for the wedding, and now she had no fiancé either.

Broodingly she looked at the immaculately painted shiny black door. Once she opened it and went in she would be walking into a completely new life. Taking a retrograde step to a stage in her career she had thought she had left behind her years ago.

She was thirty-two years old. Too old to be going back to the bottom of the heap. But then, it was her own fault. *She* was the one who was responsible for her failure. She knew that.

'You failed because you took on too many charity cases,' Bevan had told her brutally when she had broken down in tears as she had told him the news that her accountant had told her that she could no longer go on. That she must cease business and that if she was lucky—very lucky—she might just...just be able to sell both properties for sufficient to clear the outstanding mortgages.

Was that it? *Was* it because she had perhaps unwisely taken on too many cases which, while worthwhile, she had always known would never pay their way? Or was it because she was simply not a good enough solicitor, that she had not worked hard enough, that she did not have the drive...the skill...the ability to attract the kind of clients she had so desperately needed to build up her cash flow? The kind of clients that the Daniel Jeffersons of this world seemed to have in abundance, she reflected miserably.

And why not? When you had been fêted by every heavyweight national paper there was, when every serious magazine had run articles on you, and every pseudo-current-affairs programme had promoted and praised you, you would be inundated with people who wanted to give you their business.

As the old saying had it, nothing succeeded like success.

Which was why, in the middle of the worst recession for decades, Jefferson & Horwich were taking on new staff... which was why she was here, standing numbly on the doorstep of these premises, knowing that she ought to be grateful to whatever streak of compassion it had been which had persuaded Richard Horwich to take her on.

She was grateful, of course. But she was also angry, bruised, hurt and most of all bitterly aware of the way in which her failure contrasted with Daniel Jefferson's success.

And he was only thirty-seven, five years older than she was herself, unmarried, good-looking—at least if the Press photographs of him were to be believed. She hadn't seen him on television. She had been too busy trying to clear up the financial mess which had once been her business, bargaining with the building society and the bank for more time, until she had managed to find buyers for her properties. *Her* properties... their properties more like. Thank goodness they were now off her hands and both her mortgages repaid. At least she no longer had that problem to keep her awake at night.

No... but she also had no home of her own, and the unwelcome knowledge that she was having to go back to the beginning and start all over again. She grimaced bitterly to herself. No doubt she would look wonderful in her expensive, silly designer suit, grovelling to the partners, and being asked to make tea by the junior clerks.

Stop it. Stop it, she warned herself. Stop feeling sorry for yourself.

She took a deep breath and pushed open the door. Behind her, in the square, she heard a man wolf-whistle, probably at some passing young girl who had nothing more to worry her than which of her admirers she was going to go out with next, she reflected dejectedly.

As she disappeared inside the building, the man who had whistled turned and grinned at his companion.

'Very tasty, Mr Jefferson. I don't think I've seen that one before. New, is she?'

'It looks like it,' Daniel Jefferson agreed non-committally as he waited for the stallholder to weigh out the cheese he had been buying.

He was going to see old Tom Smith this afternoon. Tom was still worrying about what would happen to his cottage and his bit of land when he died. He had no direct heirs, only several distant relatives on his wife's side, and he was concerned because he wanted to make sure that young Larry Barker, the local teenager who had been so good about doing his shopping for him and calling round to give him a hand with his garden, should not go unrewarded for all his kindness.

Tom was very partial to their creamy local cheese, and so Daniel had stopped to buy him some.

So Charlotte French had actually turned up, had she? He had had his doubts when Richard had told him he had offered her the job.

He had read her CV, of course, and he was still not sure how well if at all she would settle down with them. That suit she had been wearing, for one thing... personally he didn't mind how a woman or a man for that matter chose to dress, but unfortunately some of their clients did not hold the same views.

Despite all the publicity of the Vitalle court case, the majority of their business came from the same rather conservative and traditional segment of the population it always had come from. It was just that now they had a lot more of it, and extremely short-skirted, South Molton Street suits would not be the type of thing they would expect from a woman solicitor. At least not if they were to take her seriously.

He sighed a little as he crossed the square. He knew from her qualifications just how intelligent she was, but...

A pretty, smiling receptionist welcomed Charlotte when she walked in. She obviously remembered her from her interview and offered immediately to show her where she would be working and where the cloakroom was.

'Oh, but is it all right for you to leave the front desk?' Charlotte asked her uncertainly.

The girl smiled back at her.

'Oh, yes, Mr Horwich said I was to show you where you'd be working when you arrived.

'I'm Ginny, by the way,' she introduced herself, stepping out from behind her desk.

'That's Mr Horwich's room on the left,' she told Charlotte, indicating one of the several closed doors off the corridor. 'And this one is Mr Jefferson's.'

Charlotte gave it a brief antagonistic glance. She had no doubt at all which of the partners had the most expensively equipped and luxurious office space.

'And this is your office,' Ginny told her, stopping so unexpectedly at a door immediately down the corridor from Daniel Jefferson's that Charlotte almost bumped into her.

Her office. That puzzled her a little, since she had been expecting to be sharing an office with several other junior solicitors from the way the work had been described to her. It must just be Ginny's way of describing things, she decided as Ginny opened the door for her, but as soon as she walked into the room she immediately recognised that it was equipped for only one person.

She hesitated uncertainly and looked at Ginny.

'Are you sure...? I mean, I don't think...I thought I'd be sharing an office with other people.'

'Oh.' Ginny looked confused. 'Well, Mr Horwich said to show you in here. Oh, and he said to tell you that he wouldn't be in this morning, but that Mr Jefferson would explain everything to you.'

Charlotte's heart sank. She glanced round the surprisingly spacious and very comfortably furnished office with its window overlooking the town square, and suddenly her earlier anger deserted her, leaving her feeling frighteningly vulnerable and nervous.

'I'd better get back to the main desk,' Ginny told her. 'Mitzi brings the coffee round at about ten-thirty, but if you want a drink in the meantime there's a machine in the staff-room. That's up on the top floor. Mr Jefferson had it all kitted out so that we can eat our lunch there if we want. There's a snooker table up there and a small kitchen.

'Last year we made up two snooker teams. Men versus women, and the women won.' She gave a small giggle, and then when Charlotte didn't respond she flushed and said uncertainly, 'Well, if you're sure there's nothing you need...'

Charlotte smiled automatically and shook her head, watching as the door closed behind her.

No, there was nothing she needed. If you discounted her own business, her own home, her self-respect, her pride, her future and her fiancé.

Idly she noticed the way she had put Bevan last. Had she always known that he would turn out to have feet of clay? That when it came to it he would not want to stand by her...that he had only wanted her while she was successful, while she enhanced his own image of himself? Had he *ever* loved her as he had claimed to do? And, even worse, had she really ever loved him—the way her father and her mother loved one another, for instance?

She moved over to the window and stood looking down into the square; a man was approaching the office door. He was tall and broad-shouldered, his thick dark brown hair glinting in the sunshine, and he moved energetically, lithely.

He was wearing an extremely conservative dark blue suit. She could see the crisp white edge of his cuff beneath the sleeve of his jacket. It was the kind of suit worn by a professional man. An accountant...a solicitor... Her heart gave a small fierce bound as he paused on the step and then looked up towards her window, almost as though he was aware of her scrutiny.

She recognised him immediately, of course, even though the only photographs she had seen of him had been grainy and flat. In the flesh she was much more physically aware of the strength of maleness, of his bone-structure, the strength and the power of him.

The suit he was wearing might be that of a traditional conservative man, but the body beneath it was unequivocally tough and male.

She took a hasty step back into the room, her face flushing as she pushed angry fingers into her hair, flipping it back off her face.

Her hair was the only thing she had refused to change when Bevan had insisted on helping her to update herself. It was straight and thick, with the glossy sheen of good health, its dark red colour completely natural, although people sometimes refused to believe it. She wore it in a shoulder-length bob, its silky richness in striking contrast to her pale skin and blue-green eyes.

Bevan had wanted her to have expensive courses of sunbed treatment to tan her skin, complaining that being so pale was unfashionable and unattractive, but she had always refused, pointing out to him the dangers that pale-skinned people like herself suffered from over-exposure to either natural or artificial tanning rays.

Perhaps she should have seen the warning signs then and recognised that Bevan wanted her for the image he believed she could project rather than for the person she actually was. She had certainly discovered very quickly that, once the image, the trappings of success, had gone, Bevan had gone as well.

All right, so maybe once she had recovered from the shock she had found that her pride was more hurt than her heart, but even so... It would be a long time before she trusted a member of the male sex romantically again.

What galled her the most was that Bevan had been the one to pursue her, showering her with flowers, flattering her with outrageous compliments. And at the same time trying to change her, she reminded herself wryly.

Her parents and her sister believed she was better off without him and she knew that they were right. Like the practice, her house, her expensive car, Bevan was a luxury she could no longer afford.

At least the only debt she had outstanding now was her bank overdraft. The *only*. Her mouth twisted a little, worry shadowing her face, her full lips tightening as she fought to control her feelings.

She had resisted fiercely at first when her parents had insisted on her living at home rent free; to have to return home to live in the first place at her age was galling, almost humiliating, despite the fact that she loved and got on well with her family, but, as they had gently pointed out, she had a large overdraft to repay and it was silly to have to spend money on rented accommodation while bank interest rates were so high.

Even the small second-hand car she was now using to travel the fifteen or so miles to this, her new job, had been provided by her father. Tears pricked her eyes briefly as she remembered how ashamed and miserable she had felt when he had given it to her. It wasn't that she particularly regretted losing the bright red BMW sports model she had previously been driving. In point of fact she had come to find it too ostentatious and had felt acutely uncomfortable driving it. No, what hurt was knowing that she had failed; that she was as dependent on her parents as she had been as a student; perhaps even more so.

Not that either they or Sarah, her elder sister, had done anything to suggest that they felt anything but sympathy for her, but sometimes even sympathy was hard to bear.

She felt so guilty, she recognised, and so ashamed. She had allowed herself to be carried away by Bevan's grand schemes without thinking them through properly. She had behaved foolishly and over-confidently and she had no one to blame for her present plight but herself.

But what hurt most of all was that anyone knowing what had happened to her must surely suspect her of being professionally incompetent in some way, and, even at the same time as she was fiercely grateful to Richard Horwich for giving her this job, she was almost resentful in some ways of what she suspected must have been a charitable impulse on his part.

With so many newly qualified solicitors looking for jobs, what had made him take on *her*, someone who had already shown how inefficient she was?

Her father had told her that she was too hard on herself; that she had simply, like others, ridden the crest of a financial wave which had retreated, leaving her high and dry. Maybe, but not everyone had been caught out by the roller-coaster of the sharp rise in the property market and its subsequent downturn.

Look at Daniel Jefferson, for instance. Her heart sank a little. She just hoped that she wouldn't have to come into too much contact with him. It was perhaps illogical of her to feel so . . . so antagonistic towards him, so resentful almost, and it was also unlike her, but her normal good humour seemed to have become eroded over the last six months or so. She felt raw and vulnerable, unable to stop herself repeatedly going over and over what had happened, wishing she had seen what was coming and protected not just herself but those of her clients to whom she had given her services free of charge as well. Yes, it was a great pity she had not had the foresight that Daniel Jefferson seemed to exhibit to such spectacular effect. He obviously, unlike her, had an eye for a successful cause, she decided moodily.

Look at the way he had taken on the huge Vitalle conglomerate and achieved such a spectacular success . . .

She heard a door opening and the sound of someone moving about in the adjacent office, and quickly sat down at her own desk. Daniel Jefferson had obviously arrived to start on his day's work.

What would it be today? she wondered bitterly. Some high-profile court case that would win him further acclaim; the preparation perhaps for a television interview? She had read in one of the papers how impressed the Press had been by the way he had handled his interviewers. Some people were like that, courting publicity, thriving on it. She remembered the small humiliating piece she had seen in the local paper describing the closing-down of *her* practice, pointing her out as one of the victims of the recession.

She had to put the past behind her, her father had told her gently, adding that there was no disgrace in having tried and failed; that he would rather she'd had the courage to do that and to admit her failure than had opted for the safety of a job in some large corporation.

But Charlotte couldn't help remembering how proud her parents had been of her when she had first qualified. Somehow now she felt she had no right to their pride, and that she certainly had no right to the respect and trust of her colleagues.

While she was lost in these unhappy thoughts her office door opened. She tensed, blinking away the tears that had been threatening and struggling to stand up, cursing as she did so her straight, too short skirt.

'Oh, Mr Horwich——' she began, and then stopped, because it wasn't Richard Horwich who was standing there, Richard Horwich whom she had naturally expected—forgetting Ginny's words, in her state of confusion—to seek her out to tell her exactly what her duties were going to be. It was Daniel Jefferson.

CHAPTER TWO

'I'M SORRY,' Charlotte began to apologise, cursing herself for not looking at him properly before addressing him by the wrong name.

'That's all right,' Daniel Jefferson told her easily. He was smiling at her, she noticed, a nice warm smile which for some reason increased her resentment of him, and her discomfort with herself.

'I'm sorry I wasn't here when you arrived. I was delayed on the way this morning, but Ginny will have shown you where everything is. I've arranged with Margaret Lewis, who's in charge of our trainee solicitors, to come down from upstairs at half-past ten to take you up to the nursery to introduce you to them.'

'The nursery?'

He smiled again.

'Sorry. That's what we call the room where the young trainees we have here work. Partially because they are trainees and partially because they're housed on the top floor in what were at one time, when this was a private house, the actual nurseries.'

He stopped speaking and looked assessingly at her. Charlotte was immediately self-consciously aware of the almost brash Londonness of her appearance, and only just managed to resist tugging at the hem of her skirt. Was it her imagination or did a small smile really curl the corners of his mouth as he glanced at her? She could feel her skin beginning to burn.

It was all very well for him, she decided bitterly, with his expensive hand-tailored suit; she doubted that he had ever been so hard up that he couldn't afford to buy himself clothes, even chain-store clothes, never mind the kind of things he was wearing right now. Well, let him deride her if he liked; she didn't care. Only she knew that she did. Just as she cared that *he* was the one who was standing here instructing her rather than Richard Horwich...just as she cared that she had apparently been isolated from the rest of the staff and put in an office adjacent to his own.

Why? Was it because despite the apparent warmth of that smile he had really not wanted her here on the staff? Had he perhaps even objected to his partner's hiring someone like her...a failure...a person who had not made the same resounding success of her career that he had so patently made of his?

Had she been put here in this solitary office on his instructions so that he could monitor her work...so that he could keep a check on her, because he did not trust her professionally? She suspected that she had.

Her pride, already lacerated by what she had endured, stung bitterly under this fresh assault.

'Do you think you'll be comfortable in here?' he asked her now. 'I know you're used to working on your own, so hopefully you won't find the isolation too much of a bugbear. Of course, normally the communicating door will be open.'

He nodded to a door set into the wall, which Charlotte belatedly realised must connect his office with hers.

Her bitterness and her resentment nearly choked her as she listened to him. Did he really think he actually needed to *watch* her while she worked?

She could feel her fingers curling into her palms, her nails digging into her hands as she fought the temptation to tell him what he could do with his job. She must not, could not, give way to that temptation. She tried to concentrate on that awful burdensome overdraft, on the kindness and generosity of her parents. She was not in a position where she could afford to turn her back on a job... any job... no matter how much she might detest its provider.

Not that *he* had actually given her the job. She could just imagine it now, she decided bitterly. She could just visualise what must have happened when Richard Horwich had announced that he had offered the job to her.

Richard would have had to show him her CV, of course, and it was all there... she had held nothing back, feeling that it would be dishonest to do so.

During the interview Richard had questioned her very closely about the failure of her practice, and she had answered him frankly and honestly.

She could well imagine how angry a man like Daniel Jefferson must have been when he had learned she had been offered and had accepted the job.

He was speaking to her again and she forced herself to concentrate, her face an icy mask of remoteness as she listened to him.

'I've prepared a list of the cases I most urgently need your help with. I thought it might help if you spend a few days familiarising yourself with the files. They cover quite a wide spread of things.

'I don't know whether or not Richard explained it to you, but this was originally a small country practice. No one here has ever specialised in one particular field. We prefer to deal with whatever comes our way—rather like GPs. It's my belief anyway that a good spread of work makes for a far more interesting work-load, and where we feel that something is beyond our scope we either refer the client on, or, if we feel we can do so, we take it on with the proviso that the client can seek other advice if he or she feels that we aren't doing a good job for them. It may be old-fashioned but it suits us, and I've found I'm not too keen on specialising in one particular field.'

Charlotte could feel her face burning. Did he have to remind her of her own folly in concentrating on all that conveyancing? She wanted to tell him that she had had no alternative; that she had simply not had the time to expand her field of operations...not with the property market so active and then with all the work she had taken on without any payment because she had felt the cause to be worthwhile.

Bevan had been furious with her about that. They had argued about it constantly, but she had pointed out to him that it was *her* time and that she had the right to give it freely if she wished. And even if she had not made any money she had had the gratification of knowing that she had been able to help people who otherwise would have had no chance at all of getting justice. Going to law was an expensive business, and not everyone was eligible for legal aid.

'This is a new departure for me,' Daniel Jefferson was saying. 'I've never worked in such close collaboration with anyone else before, apart from when I was newly qualified, when I worked for my father. He's retired now, of course.

'However, I have to admit with the work-load I have at the moment I do need a qualified assistant.'

An assistant! *She* had been employed as Daniel Jefferson's assistant. Charlotte bit the inside of her mouth to prevent the sharp protest she could feel bubbling in her throat erupting vocally. Nothing had been said to her about working exclusively for Daniel Jefferson when she was offered the job. On the contrary, she had assumed that she would be one of a team of junior qualified solicitors working for the practice in much the same way as qualified solicitors worked for the legal departments of large companies. They would, she had imagined, do all the dirty work while Daniel Jefferson creamed off the glory.

To discover that she was going to be working exclusively for him and under his direct control had come as a very unpleasant shock.

The temptation to challenge him to reveal the truth instead of cloaking it with pseudo-flattery, and to admit that, far from believing she could be of any real help to him, his real purpose in having her installed here in the office next to his own was because he simply did not trust her almost overwhelmed her.

It galled her more than she could bear to admit to realise what had happened. If only she could afford to give in to the demands of her pride, to tell him that she had changed her mind and that she no longer wanted his job and to walk out of here with her head held high.

But she couldn't. She had no option but to grit her teeth and give him a frosty little smile.

She was, after all, a mere employee...and *he* was the mighty Daniel Jefferson, and if he dictated that she was to spend her working life making coffee and posting letters there was damn all she could do about it.

All at once the misery and the frustration of the last few humiliating months boiled up inside her in a fierce surge of emotion directed at the man standing opposite her.

It was all right for him. He, no doubt, had never put a foot wrong, never made a mistake, and he had certainly never suffered the humiliation of losing almost everything...career...home... lover...

Not that she and Bevan had actually been lovers in the physical sense, oddly enough. After his passionate and fervent pursuit of her he had become so engrossed in reorganising her career and her image that somehow there had never seemed to be any time for them to actually become lovers. Whenever they went out, it had always been with a crowd of Bevan's friends, high-profile men and women from the same world he himself inhabited, who talked coolly of burn-out and 'yuppie flu' and who seemed to take the view that finding time to develop personal relationships was somehow something that did not fit into their plans for their lives.

Charlotte had gone along with it because ... because Bevan had swept her off her feet, she admitted miserably.

She heard Daniel Jefferson asking if there was anything she needed.

If there was anything she needed ... Yes, she needed her self-respect back, she thought bitterly. She needed to salve her pride, to feel that people believed in her, that they trusted her professional ability. She needed all those things and more, but she was not going to get them from this man.

She gave him another cold, tight smile.

'No, there's nothing I need,' she told him carefully. She fully understood what he had said to her. If he would give her the list of files he wanted her to study ...

She was damned if she was going to ask him where to find the files, she reflected ten minutes later.

The list had apparently been on his desk and when he had opened the communicating door so that he could go and collect it she had been surprised to discover that his office was not a bit as she had imagined. The furniture was slightly old-fashioned, comfortable easy chairs either side of a fireplace, a heavy partners' desk in front of the window and, most incongruously, a large wooden box of children's toys in one corner.

'I find them useful when I'm dealing with divorce cases,' he told her, seeing her look at them. 'Very often if I'm acting for the woman she brings her children with her. It helps to distract them.'

What she hadn't seen in his office, though, had been any evidence of any filing cabinets.

Perhaps she could ask this Margaret Lewis when she met her, or perhaps she could ask Ginny the receptionist.

The communicating door was still open. Charlotte longed to close it, to shut herself off from the man working in the adjacent room, the man who trusted her so little that he had had her placed here under his visual jurisdiction, but even such a small choice as closing a door was not hers to make, she fumed bitterly. She was an employee now, dependent on the whims and the commands of others.

At half-past ten she heard a knock on her outer office door. When she got up to answer it the woman standing outside introduced herself as Margaret Lewis.

She was in her fifties, tall with thick strong hair and a warm smile.

If she shared Daniel Jefferson's lack of faith in Charlotte's professional competence she certainly wasn't betraying it, and as she accompanied her up the stairs Charlotte felt herself begin to relax slightly, for the first time that morning.

'We're quite a small, close-knit unit here,' Margaret told her as they went upstairs. 'I like to think that it comes from the firm's originally being started by a woman.'

'A woman!'

Charlotte paused on the stairs to stare at her.

Margaret smiled.

'Yes. Lydia Jefferson started up in practice here just after she had qualified, when she was unable to get work with any established practice. A very adventurous step for a woman in those days.'

'Lydia Jefferson?' Charlotte questioned. 'Then she must have been... Was she related to Daniel Jefferson in some way?'

'His great-aunt,' Margaret confirmed. 'She had been retired for several years when I first came to work as an office junior, but she still took a very strong interest in the practice. In fact it was she who first encouraged me to take my own articles and to qualify. She and Daniel were very close. When he was quite small, still at junior school, she used to bring him down here with her sometimes.

'She had very strong views on women's rights to control their own lives and she was vehement in her support of the underdog. Daniel is very like her in that. Much more so than his father, who, although kind, was much more the traditional stereotype of the country solicitor.

'Daniel was a brilliant student and many people thought he should have opted to become a barrister, but he was always determined that he wanted to work here, continuing the tradition established by his aunt.'

'But surely now with all the publicity surrounding the Vitalle case he must at least be tempted to take advantage of his success and perhaps move the practice to London?'

Margaret shook her head.

'Oh, no, Daniel would never do that,' she told Charlotte calmly. She said it so positively and with such faith and affection that Charlotte felt her resentment against Daniel Jefferson surge rebelliously inside her. It was all right for him. He had had everything handed to him on a plate. All he had had to do was to qualify and then to step into the comfortable world waiting for him. A world laboured for by a woman...

A woman who had succeeded as she had not, and against far greater odds, Charlotte reminded herself miserably as they reached the top of the stairs and Margaret Lewis opened a door on the landing.

Inside the large sunny room eight people sat at desks working. The room buzzed with the hum of computers and electronic equipment. All along one of the shorter walls were racks containing the familiar packages of papers and legal briefs tied with pink ribbon.

It was obvious immediately that the people in the room were extremely busy and yet the atmosphere was one of relaxed happiness, a young woman leaning over the shoulder of a male colleague, teasing him about something as she helped him with a query.

There was, Charlotte recognised, a bright-eyed quality and an enthusiasm about the occupants of this room that said how much they enjoyed their work, and there was also an alertness about them, an eagerness that she recognised as the kind of enthusiasm possessed by those who were the best of their peer group.

Without knowing any of them, she immediately knew that these trainees were all of them high achievers, quick, intelligent, hard-working, much as she had once been herself, but they had something she recognised that she had never really had: they were free of the anxiety that had plagued her almost from the moment she had set up her own practice.

If they knew about her professional history they were certainly not showing it, as Margaret introduced them to her and they reacted with what appeared to be genuine warmth.

One or two of the boys eyed her short skirt appreciatively, but no one displayed any antagonism or unpleasantness towards her.

'Bless 'em,' Margaret commented after she had closed the office door and was standing on the landing with Charlotte. 'They're a hard-working lot, but inclined to get a little high-spirited at times. Daniel believes in giving them as much responsibility as they can handle without overburdening them, and I must admit it's a recipe they seem to thrive on. What we prefer to do is to assign someone to a specific case, so that he or she can see the whole thing through rather than merely acting as a clearing house for the mundane background work.

'When you come to start work on Daniel's files you'll find inside the cover the name of the trainee assigned to that case, and any work you want doing you can either instruct the trainee concerned direct or, if you prefer, you can route your instructions through me.

'I realise that for the next few days, until you find your feet, you're going to be tied to your desk and the files, but once you're properly settled in it might be nice to have lunch together one day.'

'Yes, I'd like that,' Charlotte told her with genuine enthusiasm. 'There is one thing you could help me with,' she added. 'Where exactly do I find the files?'

Margaret smiled at her.

'Come with me.'

As she headed back downstairs she told Charlotte that when Lydia Jefferson had first decided to set up her own practice she had bought this house with a small legacy, and thanks in the main to Daniel's insistence it had stayed much as it was rather than being converted into a modern soulless environment behind a classic façade. 'However, as we've expanded we've grown progressively short of space, and the files or at least Daniel's files are now housed in what originally was a large walk-in airing-cupboard.

'Here they are,' she told Charlotte as they stopped on the next landing. She opened a door into a small oblong room, its walls lined with shelves filled with files.

'Dead files are stored in the basement. These are only current cases.

'We operate a simple system. They are kept here in alphabetical order, and if you find that one is missing chances are either that Daniel has it out or that one of the trainees is the culprit. I have tried to institute a system whereby everyone logs the files they take out, but I'm afraid so far it's proving a little difficult to implement.

'If there's anything you want to know, or any help you need, just give me a ring, or pop up and see me. I'm on extension 241,' she told Charlotte.

Thanking her, Charlotte headed back to her own office. At least *Margaret* wasn't antagonistic towards her, but perhaps that was because as yet she did not know the truth about her.

As she stepped into her office Charlotte heard Daniel call out to her.

'Could you come into my office for a moment, please, Charlotte?'

Reluctantly she did so.

He was seated behind his desk, and while she stood in front of him, seething with resentment and misery, she was painfully aware of the contrast between them.

He looked up, smiling at her; a smile he had no doubt used to good effect for the television screens, she reflected sourly. Surely his teeth were too white...too perfect...but then she noticed that one of his front ones was slightly chipped. Oddly that cheered her up a little. So Mr Perfect wasn't entirely perfect after all.

'Here's an addition to the list of the files I'd like you to familiarise yourself with,' he told her. In order to take the list from him she had to step closer to his desk, so close that she caught the faint clean scent of his skin. He wasn't wearing aftershave; that was quite definitely merely soap she could smell. She scowled. One of the things she had never wholly cared for about Bevan was his addiction to a particularly strong male cologne. Nothing she had been able to say to him had ever convinced him that she found it more of a turn-off than a turn-on.

'Help yourself to a cup of coffee,' she heard Daniel telling her, 'and then pull up a chair. I'll give you a brief résumé of each of these cases, and then I'd like you to read through the files and give me your professional opinion of the strengths and weaknesses of each case.'

Fortunately she had her back to him as he spoke, having turned at his first words to see where she was supposed to get her coffee from. A coffee filter jug and heater stood discreetly to one side of the toy box, complete with china mugs and everything else, and as she focused on it she felt her backbone stiffen. What a mammoth ego the man had, she fumed as she poured herself some coffee. What was he trying to do—test her... as though she were a child sitting a spelling test? And then swiftly on the heels of this angry thought came another and more disturbing one. What if it *was* some kind of test? If she failed it... if her judgements on his cases did not exactly coincide with his, would he use that as further means of her incompetence and seek her dismissal?

She shivered a little as she added milk to her coffee, a mental image of her most recent bank statement reminding her of how important it was that she kept this job. The salary was excellent, and it was close enough for her to be able to live at home. And no matter how much such dependence on her parents hurt her pride, there was no getting away from the fact that until she had cleared that overdraft she simply could not afford to pay rent and she most certainly could not afford a mortgage.

The bank had been very understanding; they had offered her extra time to repay the overdraft, but her pride had jibbed at that. She wanted it reduced and repaid as quickly as possible. And besides, as her father had pointed out, there was the burden of the heavy interest payments.

Schooling her features into icy blankness, she turned round and walked back to the desk.

As she sat down she was briefly and uncomfortably aware of the way her skirt rode up along her thighs, but when she darted a brief glance at Daniel Jefferson he was looking at some papers on his desk, and he didn't lift his head until she was sitting down.

As she listened to him describing each of the cases on the list she was reluctantly forced to admit that either he had a good memory for facile detail or he was deeply and genuinely involved with every case that he took on.

She preferred to think it was the former; it was after all the kind of showmanship she would have expected from someone made so much of by the media, but honesty compelled her to accept that it was probably the latter. But then, being a good solicitor did not necessarily make him a good human being, she told herself grimly.

At five to one, even though they were only halfway through the list, he stopped and told her, 'I think that's enough for one session. I have a business appointment this lunchtime and I doubt

that I'll be back before three, so I think it might
be as well if we left the rest of the list until
tomorrow.

'I don't know if you've made any arrangements
for lunch, but if not we do have a staff-room
upstairs.'

'Yes, thank you. Ginny has already told me that.'

As she spoke, her voice curt and crisp, Charlotte
was briefly conscious of the thoughtful look he gave
her. To her intense irritation she could feel herself
flushing slightly, and she knew that had her mother
been present she would have chided her for her
attitude.

She had brought some sandwiches for her lunch.
The town was well known to her, small but busy
with a very pleasant little park by the river, and she
had planned originally to have lunch there.

However, it was a cool day with a grey sky and
she had to admit that she would probably be more
comfortable in the staff-room.

She was touched when she walked back into her
office to find Ginny waiting there for her.

'It can sometimes be awkward when you're new,'
Ginny told her with a friendly smile. 'So I thought
I'd come and see if you wanted to go upstairs for
lunch.'

'Thank you. I've brought some sandwiches with
me because I wasn't sure. I had planned to eat them
by the river, but it is rather cold.'

As they walked out into the corridor a woman
was coming the other way.

She was taller, much taller than Charlotte, who
was barely five foot three, with glossy black hair

cut and permed in a dramatic style that suggested she made frequent visits to a hairdresser's. Her make-up too was immaculate, if rather overdone for Charlotte's taste. She was wearing a suit which Charlotte recognised as this season's Chanel and there was a large and very ostentatious diamond ring on her ring hand.

She gave the two women a cold sharp glance and said icily to Ginny, 'The reception desk is unattended. I'm sure Daniel won't be pleased about that.' And then she looked at Charlotte, her eyes hardening a little as her glance lingered just a little too long on Charlotte's suit. Her mouth compressed and, although she said nothing, Charlotte was left very much aware of what she thought of her appearance.

As soon as she had disappeared into Daniel's office Ginny whispered, 'That's Mrs Patricia Winters. *The* Mrs Patricia Winters... widow of the late Paul Winters.' She grinned as Charlotte looked mystified. 'He was a local man—a property millionaire. She married him when he was sixty-odd and she was twenty-three. Now he's dead and rumour has it that she's looking for a second husband and that this time she's going for the jackpot. Looks as well as wealth.' She rolled her eyes.

'Poor Daniel. They're saying upstairs in the nursery that it's a pity that solicitors aren't protected from their clients in the same way that doctors are from their patients.'

'Maybe he doesn't *want* to be protected,' Charlotte suggested. In fact it seemed to her that

Patricia Winters would be the ideal mate for a man like Daniel Jefferson.

'Oh, no, he couldn't possibly want to marry her. He's much too nice,' Ginny protested.

What was the man running here, a practice or a fan club? Charlotte wondered sourly. Well, *she* certainly wasn't going to join. Everyone else might think he was wonderful, but *she* certainly did not.

'Mrs Winters is a client, then?' she commented as she and Ginny went upstairs.

'Mm, although since her husband died she seems to need Daniel's advice far more than Paul Winters ever did when he was alive.'

As she glanced out of the window Charlotte saw that there was a large Rolls-Royce parked outside. A chauffeur was opening the door and Patricia Winters was stepping inside it. Daniel was standing beside her. So *that* was his business appointment. Nice work if you can get it, Charlotte reflected acidly.

Wherever they were going, she doubted that they would be eating sandwiches, unless they were the smoked salmon and caviare variety, combined with a bottle of champagne and consumed in the privacy of Mrs Winters's undoubtedly luxurious and very glamorous bedroom.

Abruptly Charlotte frowned, her face flushing a little as she recognised with some distaste the direction of her thoughts. Whatever she might think of Daniel Jefferson, she had no right to allow her imagination *that* particular kind of inventive licence.

CHAPTER THREE

ONE of the files she had been instructed to study would of course have to come under 'A', Charlotte reflected wryly as she glanced up towards the topmost shelf, several feet above her head, but as she chewed on her bottom lip and wondered how on earth she was supposed to get to the file she suddenly saw the step-ladders carefully stowed away in a corner.

They were the lightweight aluminium kind and easy for her to pick up and carry and open out. Anxious to collect the files and start work on reading them, she hurried up the steps, cursing under her breath as she recognised the folly of doing so in high heels and a straight skirt. She had never particularly liked heights and she realised a little queasily that in order to reach the file she wanted she was going to have to stand on the topmost step and that she would have nothing to hold on to other than the shelf itself.

Her mind filled with the horrendous mental vision of the metal rack, steps, files and all top-pling over completely as she clung to it, causing her to balance herself as carefully as she could without relying on it for support.

As she looked quickly along the rack for the file she wanted she realised that she had positioned the ladders too close to the 'AM's rather than the 'AN' section that she needed.

Trust her. Now she couldn't even do a simple job like collecting a few files efficiently. Irritated with herself and frustrated with impatience, she leaned over as far as she could, cursing under her breath as she felt her skirt pull tightly against her legs, impeding her. The file was tantalisingly close. If she could just stretch out a few more centimetres she would be able to reach it without having to go to all the bother of climbing down the steps, repositioning them and then climbing up them again.

She held her breath, stretching her body as far as she could as she reached for the file.

'What the...?'

The shock of hearing Daniel Jefferson's sharp exclamation made her turn defensively to face him, but she had forgotten her precarious position on the ladders, and as she turned she felt them rock beneath her with the unsteadiness of her own movements, and she knew that she was going to fall.

Only she didn't; instead of finding herself in an ignominious heap on the floor at Daniel Jefferson's feet, she found herself in the equally ignominious position of being held against his body as he reached out and grabbed her before she could fall.

Several equally unpalatable facts hit her at the same time: firstly that she had made a complete and absolute fool of herself and no doubt further confirmed his belief that she was not the kind of employee he wanted; secondly that as she fell she must have dislodged some of the files and that they and their contents were now lying in a puddle of papers and tape on the floor while the ladders leaned drunkenly against the shelves; and, thirdly, and most unpalatable of all, Daniel was holding her so that her breasts were virtually on a level with his eyes and, even worse, she was horribly aware of the length of dark-tight-covered thigh she was now exposing.

'It's OK, I've got you,' she heard him telling her, as if she needed telling. She had a perfectly good set of senses and they were fast relaying to her that not only had he 'got her', as he had put it, but that for some extraordinary reason her body actually seemed to rather like the sensation of his solid male warmth against it.

Impossible. She didn't even *like* the man, much less... She closed her eyes against the attack of vertigo that hit her as Daniel started to lower her to the ground, instinctively grabbing hold of his jacket-covered arms to combat her dizziness.

'Are you sure you're OK?' she heard him asking her as her feet finally touched the floor. 'That could have been quite a nasty accident. What on earth were you doing, anyway?'

Now that he had released her and stepped back from her so that he could look at her, Charlotte pushed the feelings she had experienced when he had held her to the back of her mind. Quite naturally, as well as shock, she was now also suffering from embarrassment and temper.

'I should have thought that was obvious,' she told him, ignoring the first part of his question. 'I was trying to reach a file.'

She flushed as he looked from her to the ladders leaning against the shelves.

'Mm... but surely not on those? Why didn't you use the other ladders? We had them specially designed for the top shelves.'

The *other* ladders. Charlotte swallowed, and felt her face flame as Daniel walked past her and then closed the door to the room, so that she could see in the wall space alongside the door a pair of tall aluminium ladders.

'As you can see, these have a guide rail on them, specifically to prevent the kind of accident you so nearly sustained.'

As she swallowed her humiliation and fury Charlotte ached to tell him that if *he* hadn't startled her she would not have fallen off the ladders in the first place.

'After all, this is a solicitors' practice,' he told her wryly. 'Don't you think we're well aware of the dangers of litigation should our employees damage themselves in the execution of their work?'

The room was so small and he was so tall, so...so big that suddenly there didn't seem to be enough air. Charlotte found that she was having difficulty in breathing somehow. She was aware that Daniel was watching her...that he was, in fact, she realised after one quick startled look at him, looking at her mouth.

Immediately she was filled with an irresistible need to touch her lips with her tongue-tip. Why, she asked herself savagely, to see if they're still there? Of course they are, and what you're doing is one of the oldest and most provocative come-ons there is. The kind of trick some third-rate film director might pull. Maybe so, but she still couldn't stop herself from doing it, a quick reflex action, instinctive and unstoppable.

She must be going crazy, she decided light-headedly. It must be the lack of air in the room, the shock of her near-accident. She swayed slightly on her feet and heard Daniel asking her again, 'Are you sure you're OK?'

She parted her lips to speak and then froze as he made a small, almost inaudible sound. When she looked at him his eyes were a dark glittering grey. He must have some special mesmeric powers, she thought dizzily as she tried to look away and could not. No wonder he was the darling of the media. He probably mesmerised his TV audiences in the same way that he was mesmerising her.

Angry with herself for her weakness, she closed her eyes and turned her head away, taking a deep calming breath.

When she opened her eyes again she felt no better, but at least she was no longer looking directly at him.

'I'm fine,' she told him shortly, and then, as she headed for the door, she found the will-power to say grittily, 'What a pity you managed to catch me. If you hadn't done and I'd fallen on you, injuring you, *you* could have sued *me*.'

To her surprise he laughed, and then surprised her even further by telling her, 'Lydia would have *loved* you.'

She had her hand on the door-handle when he stopped her, taking hold of her so gently but so powerfully that she could only stare up at him. She gave him a suspicious angry look, her muscles resisting him as she glared at him.

'I don't know what you think you're doing.'

He was still smiling at her, but now his smile chilled a little and his voice was crisply cool as he told her, 'I think you might want to—er—adjust your skirt before you leave.'

With that he stepped past her and opened the door, firmly closing it and leaving her shut in the small room, her face on fire as she glanced down and saw the ruched, untidy state of her skirt, and the length of thigh it exposed.

She was perilously close to angry tears as she dragged the fabric back down, and then set about tidying up the mess on the floor.

Damn him. Damn him. It was all his fault... if he hadn't startled her...

It was a further half an hour or so before she had collected the rest of the files. When she went back to her office her heart sank as she saw that the communicating door to Daniel's office was open.

He was on the telephone when she went in, and as she walked to her own desk she saw a packet of sandwiches open on his.

He had finished his call and replaced the receiver, turning towards her as he asked, 'You got the rest of the files without any problems, then?'

Her stiff, 'Yes, thank you,' should have made it plain that any kind of conversation with him was the last thing she wanted, but he seemed unaware of her coldness, adding,

'I'm just trying to snatch some lunch. I didn't get time for anything to eat earlier.'

As Charlotte turned her back on him her face burned with indignation. Did he really think she was remotely interested in the way he and his ... his client had spent their lunch-hour? She was tempted to make some derisory comment, but she reminded herself just in time that she was a mere employee, and one whose grip on her job was tenuous in the extreme.

She spent the rest of the afternoon reading through the first of the files and she was relieved when at half-past three Daniel closed the door between them, saying that he had a client interview.

'Later, once you've acquainted yourself with the contents of the files, I shall of course expect you to sit in on any relevant interviews.'

To sit in on *his* interviews, but not to conduct any of her own, Charlotte thought balefully once the door was closed. Another indication of how little he trusted her professional judgement.

At four o'clock her office door opened and Richard Horwich came in.

'I'm sorry I wasn't here to welcome you this morning,' he told her with a fatherly smile. 'Unfortunately I was in court. I'm sure you're settling in very well, though.'

'Yes... Yes, thank you. I...I didn't realise I would be working solely for Mr Jefferson.'

Richard raised his eyebrows a little at her formal 'Mr' but Charlotte noticed that he looked a little uncomfortable as he told her, 'Yes, well...I...that is... With his increased work-load, we both felt that Daniel needed his own qualified assistant.'

It was just as she had suspected, Charlotte decided. The decision to make her Daniel Jefferson's assistant had only been taken once Daniel had seen her CV and decided that she was not to be trusted to work on her own.

She wanted to protest that she was a *qualified* solicitor, not a child needing constant supervision, but she struggled to suppress the bitterness and resentment churning inside her, reminding herself of how much she needed to keep this job.

Richard had barely been gone for ten minutes when someone else knocked on Charlotte's door.

The girl who came in was pretty and very pregnant. She smiled at Charlotte and introduced herself.

'I'm Anne, Daniel's secretary, and yours of course. I had a clinic appointment this morning.' She patted her stomach and grimaced. 'I'll be glad when he or she eventually decides to arrive, I can tell you.'

'Is it... is it your first baby?' Charlotte asked her.

A little to her surprise, Anne shook her head.

'No, we already have a four-year-old, Jeremy. Peter, my husband, works from home. He's a computer analyst and he works freelance. When Jeremy was born I had planned to stay at home with him full-time, but with Peter there as well... Well, at times I found it rather claustrophobic, and with this one I definitely intend to come back after my maternity leave is up. It's not so much the money, although I must admit I enjoy that aspect of it... Not that Peter isn't generous, but it's nice to have some financial independence. No, it's the contact with other people I missed the most, but I must say that working for someone like Daniel makes it a whole lot easier. He's very understanding, very concerned about his employees.'

'I suppose he has to be, doesn't he?' Charlotte commented, and then bit her lip as she realised that her slightly acid comment was causing Anne to look rather doubtfully at her.

'Well, he has to consider his media image, doesn't he?' she added rather lamely. 'When people are in the public limelight...'

'Oh, no, Daniel isn't *that* kind of person,' Anne told her firmly. 'No, it's just the kind of man he is. He believes that happy people work far better than those who are unhappy, and I think he's right.'

Charlotte forced herself to smile, although she was gritting her teeth together when Anne left the room.

What was it about the man that sent everyone into such raptures of praise about him? He must have mesmerised them all; well, she certainly wasn't going to join his adoring fan club, she reaffirmed savagely as she picked up another file. He might deceive everyone else, but he certainly wasn't going to deceive her.

The file she was reading involved a particularly intricate and difficult case, and Charlotte was so engrossed in what she was reading that five o'clock came and went without her being aware of it.

In fact she wasn't really aware of any kind of extraneous activity at all until the communicating door opened and Daniel walked into her room.

'Still working?' He stood beside her and glanced down at the file she was reading.

'Mm...that's a complex one, isn't it? I'm not sure how it's going to work out. There is a valid claim for compensation, but how far that is going to be affected by some element of contributary negligence is hard to define. It's just gone six,' he told her gently, 'and we don't work London hours here.'

'*You're* still here,' Charlotte pointed out. Could she do nothing right? In point of fact she hadn't even realised what time it was.

'I had some things I wanted to catch up on.' He paused, and Charlotte looked up at him. For one brief unguarded moment they looked directly at one another and she was suddenly and sharply conscious of a breathless tightness in her chest, a feeling of dizzy light-headedness.

'I know it can't be easy for you,' Daniel said quietly. 'It's obvious from your CV...'

Suddenly the breathlessness was gone and Charlotte was once again acutely aware of the differences in their positions.

'That I'm a failure,' she supplied bitingly for him.

'Yes. I am well aware of that, but you needn't worry that the taint of that failure might affect you. After all, you're taking enough steps to make sure that it won't, aren't you?'

She closed the file as she spoke, standing up and saying curtly, 'It's time I left.'

She was halfway towards the door when he spoke again. 'Charlotte, I think perhaps we should talk——'

She turned to face him, unaware of the pain darkening her eyes.

'Do you?' she challenged. 'Well, *I* don't. All I want is to do my job. Nothing else. The past . . . my past has nothing to do with you or with anyone else.'

'No . . . no, of course not.'

His mouth had hardened slightly, she noticed. He was looking at her rather bleakly, and in other circumstances she might almost have thought she had disappointed him in some way.

She was still seethingly angry three-quarters of an hour later when she stopped her car in the drive to her parents' house. Why on earth did she have to work for someone like him? Someone so . . . so perfect, at least according to everyone else, that his perfection physically set her teeth on edge. Was there nothing the man had ever done wrong . . . no mistake he had ever made . . . no fault to be found with him?

But then, it was easy for him. He had stepped right into a well-established practice, taking his place at its head by virtue of birth rather than merit. And then to win the Vitalle case so dramatically . . .

As she walked towards the house her conscience niggled at her, reminding her of how hard he must have worked on the case, and of how many other practices had turned down the victims before they had actually gone to him.

It was luck, that was all. Just luck, she told herself crossly, but she knew that she was being unfair. Well, why not? He was being equally unfair to her. More so... It was all very well for him. He had no idea what it was like to fail... and to have to carry the burden of that failure.

'Well, how did it go?' Her mother pounced as she walked into the kitchen.

Charlotte shook her head. 'Don't ask.'

'Why, what's wrong?' her mother demanded anxiously.

Quickly Charlotte told her, concluding, 'He obviously doesn't trust me and that's why he's insisting on keeping me under his eye. On creating this job for me... because I'm sure that is what he's done. He obviously took one look at my CV and decided there was no way I could be trusted to deal with cases on my own. I suppose it's only what I deserve——'

'Oh, no, Charlotte, I'm sure you're wrong,' her mother protested. 'It sounds to me as though he must think very highly of you to want you working for him personally.'

Charlotte gave her mother a derisive look.

'How *can* he think highly of me? He's seen my CV. No, he obviously resents the fact that Richard Horwich has given me the job and he's determined to let me know that he doesn't trust me. He's probably afraid that I might contaminate his precious practice with my failure if I'm left to do anything by myself.'

'Oh, Charlotte,' her mother protested, 'what's happened to you? You never used to be like this. You sound so... so bitter.'

Charlotte bit down hard on her bottom lip. 'I'm sorry, Ma... It's just——'

'It's all right,' her mother told her, patting her hand, 'I do understand. Oh, by the way, it's just the two of us for supper tonight. Your father is eating at the golf club—oh, and Sarah is coming round later.'

'I'd better go upstairs and change my suit.'

Damned thing, why on earth had she ever been persuaded to buy it? It and all the rest of the expensive designer outfits hanging in her wardrobe, Charlotte fumed as she changed into jeans and a pretty, loose jumper.

She dared not tell her mother how uncomfortable she had felt, otherwise she knew what would happen. Her mother would insist on buying her some new clothes and she wasn't going to allow her to do that. She owed her parents enough as it was.

Her father had had a good job, but he was retired now and while they were reasonably comfortably off they were not well off by any means, and, besides, she simply did not want to be dependent on them.

But she *was* dependent on them... just as she was dependent on Daniel Jefferson... or rather on his job.

She had brought two of the files home with her and she had intended to spend the evening studying them. She was going to prove to him that she was competent at her job if it was the last thing she ever did.

Not that she was likely to get much work done if Sarah was going to come round.

She grinned ruefully to herself. She had always got on well with her older sister, despite the difference in their lifestyles. Sarah was happily and comfortably married with two children, and, as she had often said to Charlotte, while she was in the fortunate position of having a husband who could both afford and was quite happy for her to stay at home with their children, she intended to do so.

She liked being domesticated. She enjoyed making her own jam, and working in her small vegetable garden; she liked spending time with her children, watching them grow and develop. She was also involved with their school, giving up several days a month when she accompanied some of the classes on a variety of school outings.

Sarah might not consider herself to be 'working', but Charlotte knew that in fact she worked very hard indeed and that she was extremely adaptable and intelligent.

Sarah had been one of the few people she had felt she could be completely honest with regarding how she had felt about the failure of her business, and as she helped her mother to prepare their supper she suspected that Sarah had timed her visit deliberately to coincide with her first day at work.

Sarah arrived about an hour after supper when Charlotte was upstairs in her bedroom, with the contents of her wardrobe strewn on her bed, as she tried to find something she could wear for work that would be more comfortable and less eye-catching than today's suit.

She heard her sister coming up the stairs and opened her bedroom door.

'What on earth are you doing?' her sister demanded as she surveyed the clothes on the bed.

'Trying to find something suitable to wear for work,' Charlotte told her.

She sounded so dispirited that Sarah immediately frowned, clearing a space on the bed so that she could sit down.

'What is it, Char? What's really wrong?' she asked her. 'Is it Bevan?'

Charlotte shook her head.

'No, I realised weeks ago that I never really loved him. I was just flattered by him, if you like. I feel so angry with myself for being taken in by him . . . For letting him have so much say in my life. I've learned my lesson, though. From now on any decisions I take about my life will be made by me and only me. I feel so guilty, Sarah,' she added in a quieter tone. 'I've let Mum and Dad down, and——'

'Hey, come on. No one thinks that but you. You've nothing to feel guilty about, Char. Look, Tony has to go away for a couple of days on business. Why don't I park the kids with the parents and you and I can have a night out on the town? Well, an Italian anyway. There's a new place opened recently, and it's supposed to be very good.

'Come on,' she coaxed as Charlotte started to frown. 'It will do us both good.'

She picked up a dress off the bed and eyed it ruefully.

'Mm. I wish I was more your size. Is this really supposed to be a dress?' she added. 'It looks more like a bandage.'

'It's an Alaïa,' Charlotte told her wryly.

'Is it?' Sarah grinned at her. 'Well, it's certainly sexy... Wear it when we go out for dinner and then I can bask in the reflected glow of the attention you'll get from the waiters. Italians love a nicely shaped female behind.'

She laughed at Charlotte's expression.

'What about it? Shall we go out?'

'Oh, all right.'

'Great, I'll book the table. Anyway, tell me all about your new job. Is Daniel Jefferson as sexy in the flesh as he looks on TV? Now what have I said?' she asked as she saw the look Charlotte was giving her. 'Hey, come on. What's wrong?' she asked more gently as she saw the genuine misery in Charlotte's eyes.

'I thought I was going to be working independently... to be treated as a qualified solicitor. Now I find that I'm working for Daniel Jefferson as his personal assistant. He doesn't *want* me there, Sarah. He doesn't trust me.'

'Has he said so?' Sarah questioned.

Charlotte shook her head.

'He doesn't *need* to, it's obvious.'

'Don't you think you might just be jumping to conclusions a little bit there?' Sarah counselled her. 'Let's face it, you *have* been feeling rather down lately, looking at things through less than rose-tinted glasses.'

'It isn't that, Sarah.' She got up off the bed and started pacing her room. 'Everything he says...everything he does, just seems to reinforce the differences between us. He makes me feel so aware of my failure. It's so galling knowing that he doesn't trust my professional capabilities. If I didn't need this job so desperately——'

'Char, don't you think you could be reacting just a little bit over-sensitively?' Sarah asked her gently. 'I know you're feeling a bit raw and sore and——'

'And what? Because of that, I'm not reacting to the wonderful Daniel Jefferson the way everyone else does—it's because of *that* that I'm not filled with awe and delight at the thought of throwing myself at his feet in worshipful adoration? Oh, the whole situation is impossible, Sarah. Virtually the entire staff, from what I can see, seem to spend all their time singing his praises. It makes me feel so angry. He's had everything just handed to him on a plate. He's never come anywhere near experiencing what I've experienced, and yet he still feels that he has the right to judge me...to condemn me...'

'Char, don't you think that perhaps...well, that *you* are a little over-prejudiced against *him*...?'

Charlotte stared at her, her expression reflecting the pain of her sister's apparent betrayal. 'What do you mean?' she began defensively, but she could see exactly what Sarah did mean from the look in her eyes.

She could feel her throat clogging with angry tears.

'Oh, I see. You think it's because he's successful and I'm a failure. You think I'm jealous of him.'

'No...no, of course not,' Sarah assured her. 'And you're *not* a failure. No, I just mean that because you've been so upset by everything that's happened your judgements, your reactions, are just a little off-centre at the moment. And Char...' she added '...be honest, you *are* bound to feel just the smallest bit resentful of him, aren't you? You wouldn't be human if you didn't. There's nothing wrong in that, but it's so unlike you to allow yourself to be so prejudiced against anyone. *You've* always been the one who's striven to see the other person's point of view. And if, as you say, the rest of the staff like him...'

'*I* have to be in the wrong. Is that it? It's the way he treats me, Sarah. He doesn't trust me. He doesn't want me there.'

'But you *are* there, aren't you?' Sarah reminded her. 'And, given time, he's bound to see that he's wrong. You are sure that *he's* the one who doubts your professional ability, Char?'

'What do you mean?'

Sarah stood up. 'When Sam first had his bike he fell off it and he was afraid to get back on it. Every time he walked past it he kicked it because it had hurt him. He blamed the bike for his fall rather than admit that he was afraid to get back on it in case he fell off again.'

'Are you saying that I only have the reasoning powers of a three-year-old?' Charlotte asked her grimly.

'No. I'm just reminding you that you *are* only human.'

'Unlike Daniel Jefferson. He's perfect... Everyone says so.'

Sarah gave her a brief look. 'So you don't like him, then.'

'Like him? I hate him,' Charlotte said decisively.

Sarah raised her eyebrows as she opened the bedroom door. 'Be very careful,' she warned her with sisterly candour. 'You know what they say about hatred...'

'What?' Charlotte demanded.

'That it's akin to love.'

Sarah was laughing as she went downstairs, but Charlotte followed her with a very heavy heart.

She knew her sister. Sarah possessed a gentle, kind nature and she hated hurting anyone. Her comments about her own possible prejudice, about her jealousy, had hurt, and although Charlotte tried to push them to the back of her mind they refused to be submerged, resurfacing throughout the evening, making her feel uncomfortable and on edge.

Was it true? Was her antagonism towards Daniel based on more than her resentment at his obvious lack of faith in her? *Was* she, as Sarah had so gently suggested, actually jealous of him... jealous of his success?

It was an extremely unpalatable thought.

She had planned to have an early night, but by the time Sarah had gone and her father had returned to regale them with a shot-by-shot description of his golf match it was gone ten o'clock and Charlotte still hadn't even opened the files she had brought home with her. She was determined that, while she worked for him, Daniel was not going to have any excuse for criticising her work. She would show him that, although economically she might be a failure, as a solicitor she was just as capable and skilled as he was himself.

She worked until a sleepy glance at the clock reminded her that it was almost one in the morning. Her back ached from sitting in the chair at the kitchen table.

She closed the file she had been reading. It was another complex case and one she was rather surprised Daniel had taken up. There was no money in it, from what she could see, and certainly no prestige, and the amount of work which had so far gone into it far outweighed any return in financial terms to the practice.

If she hadn't known better she might almost have believed that Daniel had taken the case on out of kindness.

She frowned as she closed the file. Was she misjudging him? Was she to add that to the already too long list of her failings?

She got up and walked restlessly over to the sink, turning on the tap and pouring herself a glass of cold water.

He was a high-profile, successful achiever, with a media image to maintain. He was not the kind of person who gave way to charitable impulses. She had met enough men like him to know that. The men with whom Bevan had mixed.

But what if she *was* wrong? As Sarah had so gently pointed out to her, everyone else who worked for him liked and admired him.

She could feel the panic starting to bubble ominously inside her. She didn't want to be wrong, she admitted. She *wanted*, she *needed* to cling to her image of him. She *needed* her dislike of him. She needed it to protect herself...

She put down the glass, her hand trembling slightly. To protect herself from what?

She had a momentary and very disturbing mental image of his eyes darkening as he watched her, the tension in her body sharply increasing. Her mouth had gone dry. She discovered that she was touching her lips with her tongue as she had done in the filing-room. Distress burned a hot path through her body.

It was gone one o'clock in the morning. She had had an extremely traumatic day and now she was allowing her imagination to create monsters which simply did not exist.

It was time she went to bed.

CHAPTER FOUR

'CHARLOTTE, have you got a moment, please?'

Charlotte put down the file she had been reading and went through into Daniel's office.

He smiled at her as he invited her to sit down, his eyes crinkling slightly, his smile revealing the small chip on his tooth.

Was she wrong about him? *Was* Sarah right to suggest that she was being over-sensitive, over-prejudiced? She knew how much her sister loved her. Sarah had never been the type of person to be destructively critical and it was true that, the more contact she had with other members of the staff, the more she was forced to recognise the very high esteem in which all of them held Daniel; the men as well as the women.

Anne was also in the room and she too smiled at Charlotte as she walked in. She had obviously been taking dictation, and now she picked up her pad and removed her coffee-cup.

'I have to go out and see a client this afternoon. He wants to make a new will. He's bedridden and can't come into the office. I'd like you to come with me.'

'Not John Balfour?' Anne commented with a wry smile.

'Yes, I'm afraid so,' Daniel agreed.

'That makes the fifth time he's changed his will in the last eight months.'

'He gets lonely,' Daniel told her. 'None of his family lives close enough to visit him, and, while physically he's very well looked after, he misses the stimulation of having someone to talk to.'

'Someone to argue with, you mean,' Anne derided. 'And, if he's that lonely, there are all sorts of local organisations who would gladly visit him.'

'He's very proud, Anne,' Daniel told her gently. 'He doesn't want what he thinks of as "charity" of any kind. This way, by saying that he wants to change his will, or by complaining that I didn't follow his last set of instructions correctly, his pride is salved because my visit is for business purposes.'

'Yes, and you'll extend it for at least double the length of time it should have taken and you'll charge him next to nothing,' Anne said, smiling at him. 'Sometimes I think you should have been a psychologist and not a solicitor.'

'It costs nothing to be aware of people's vulnerabilities and needs. After all, we all need one another's help at one time or another in our lives.'

Charlotte digested his comment in silence. Privately she could not imagine this man ever needing anything from anyone, but she couldn't deny the genuine conviction she could hear in his voice.

She tried to imagine Bevan or any of his 'friends' doing what Daniel was doing, but her imagination simply could not stretch that far. In Bevan's life, everything was profit-related. Including her, and once their relationship had begun to show a loss . . .

She didn't regret losing Bevan, but it still hurt that she had ever been idiotic enough to be taken in by him.

'You'll like John,' Daniel told Charlotte, adding cryptically, with a look that suddenly made her tinglingly aware of how very male he was, how very physically compelling...even if *she* was the last person to allow herself to be impressed by his kind of male sensuality, 'You're both fighters.'

A fighter! Her! How could he think so? She was all too bitterly aware of how cravenly she had given up at the very first obstacle she had had to confront. But what option had she had? If she had persisted in staying in business she would have risked betraying her clients' trust. She had owed it to *them* to admit her failure and to advise them to seek the counsel of other more sensible and financially aware solicitors.

Perhaps she could have kept on going for another few months, deceiving her clients by pretending that all was going well. The insurance cover she had had would have indemnified them against any financial losses they might have suffered, but there had been no way they could have been insured against the loss of time that would have occurred, and she had not felt able to take that kind of risk. Bevan had derided her for that. He took risks every day, huge financial risks involving millions of pounds. That was what life was all about, and the element of danger it involved simply heightened one's sense of satisfaction when one pulled off a clever deal.

She was not like that, though. She was too cautious.

'I'm afraid it will mean your missing part of your lunch-hour,' Daniel was saying now.

'It doesn't matter.' Charlotte was aware of how stiff and defensive she sounded. Anne had left the room now and she was standing in front of Daniel's desk, clutching the file she was holding as though it was some form of protection...of armour almost, but armour against what?

There was a file on Daniel's desk, and she looked at it, automatically tensing as she recognised Patricia Winters's name.

When he realised she was looking at it Daniel moved his arm as though to cover it, and Charlotte was filled with a fresh surge of angry defensiveness. Why did he feel it was necessary to conceal the file from her? What possible harm could she do, simply by looking at it?

'How are you getting on with the files?' he asked her.

Immediately she tensed. 'I'm halfway through them,' she told him sharply.

His eyebrows lifted thoughtfully. 'Are you? You must be an extremely fast reader.'

Charlotte felt her face start to burn. What was he implying? That she had merely skipped through them without giving them enough attention? No doubt if she had told him that she had only read the first two of them he would have remarked not on her thoroughness but on her slowness.

No...no matter how much kindness he might display towards others, he most definitely did not like her.

But then, why should he? she asked herself as she went back to her own office. After all, he had obviously not wanted her; he obviously saw her as a burden, a responsibility. Every time he saw her he was probably cursing himself for allowing Richard to interview and employ her.

Perhaps, in his shoes, she would feel exactly the same way. After all, an employee who could not be trusted to do her job, who had to be supervised all the time, was hardly an asset.

Bitter tears burned the back of her eyes as she sat down at her own desk. She blinked them fiercely away.

'We'll leave in half an hour,' Daniel had said. She picked up the large shoulder-bag which doubled as her documents case and checked inside it to make sure she had a notepad and a couple of pens. She had no idea why Daniel wanted her to accompany him—probably because he didn't trust her in the office on her own, she reflected acidly. Why, she might actually answer the phone and speak to a client...

'Ready?'

The sound of Daniel's voice startled her. She hadn't heard him get up and come through into her office. She had been too engrossed in what she was reading.

Of course, he would have to come and stand right beside her, making her feel acutely self-conscious, so much so that when she pushed back her chair, instead of getting up in one smooth elegant movement, she did so in a series of flustered, uncoordinated jerks, almost knocking the file off her desk and then dropping her jacket.

'Here, let me.'

She tensed as Daniel retrieved her jacket before she could reach it, holding it out to her so that she had no option but to allow him to help her on with it.

The sun shining into her office highlighted the thinness of her silk shirt, turning it almost transparent. Beneath it she was wearing a plain but equally thin silk bra, and as she glanced down at herself she was suddenly acutely conscious of what little the two thin layers of silk did to disguise the darkness of the aureolae of flesh surmounting her breasts.

Sexual provocativeness wasn't a part of her nature and never had been. She was vaguely aware that a certain type of man found her small but very feminine type of build attractive, but she had never tried to accentuate her body's desirability, deeming such behaviour undignified and unnecessary—and yet now she was suddenly very uncomfortably conscious that, to a man's eyes, the fineness of her bra and her blouse might seem to be some sort of 'come-on', some sort of deliberate ploy to draw attention to her body.

As she felt the warmth of Daniel's hands through her jacket she quickly shrugged herself into it, pulling away from him as she mumbled an unsteady, 'Thank you.'

'You're welcome,' he told her, and as she turned round she saw that he was regarding her with a thoughtful gravity.

Had he seen the sudden swelling tension of her nipples which she herself had been so sharply aware of? She prayed that he had not. It was not merely humiliating that her body should have reacted in such a way, it was also incomprehensible. She had not had the least difficulty in the past in working with male colleagues. She had never considered herself to be the kind of woman who was physically vulnerable to the proximity of an attractive man.

And Daniel *was* attractive, not even she could deny that. There was something about him, a combination of extreme maleness allied to an unexpected warmth of personality, that was strongly compelling.

No wonder Patricia Winters was supposed to want him as her second husband. *Would* they marry? They would certainly make a very striking high-profile couple.

Reminding herself that his personal relationships were not her concern, she picked up her bag, glad that the soft downward swing of her hair concealed her expression from him.

She felt both guilt and discomfort at her body's reaction to him, mixed with apprehension and anger that he might have witnessed it.

'My car's parked outside,' he told her as they walked through the reception area.

As he opened the door for her the only car which Charlotte could see was an extremely old-fashioned but immaculately polished Jaguar saloon with a maroon body.

'This was my great-aunt Lydia's car,' he told her as he unlocked the door. 'She left it to me. I don't drive it all the time, but John and Lydia were good friends, and he will be able to see it from his window.'

Charlotte said nothing.

The car had leather seats, the leather worn and cracked in places. The anger and resentment she had initially felt on realising his mistrust of her was rapidly being replaced by a sense of forlorn misery, as though she was being excluded from an enviable magic circle, an onlooker to a party she would never be asked to join. He had so much compassion for everyone else; why, then, couldn't he have some for her?

She gritted her teeth. She didn't *want* his compassion, she reminded herself. And she certainly didn't need it.

He drove carefully and well, as she might have expected, and as she watched the easy controlled way in which he changed gear she was abruptly reminded of a London girlfriend's comment that you could tell a lot about the way a man would make love from the way he handled his car.

Bevan had driven his Porsche far too fast, crunching the gears, racing the engine, driving up far too close behind other drivers and then weaving in and out of the traffic, impatient and inconsiderate of other road users. Just the opposite from Daniel, in fact, who had slowed down to allow a young mother to cross the road.

The home where John Balfour lived was a few miles outside the town. As they drove up, Charlotte saw several elderly people either walking or sitting in the garden, well wrapped up against the wind, and once they were inside the building through an open door she could see into a large comfortable lounge, where some people were playing cards while others chatted or watched television.

'John has a wheelchair and he could join the others if he wished, but he's the stubborn type and he can't see how much pleasure and companionship his stubbornness is depriving him of.'

'Perhaps he *prefers* his own company,' Charlotte suggested, driven for some reason to defend him.

'Perhaps,' Daniel agreed as they walked up the stairs.

But then, if he did prefer his own company he wouldn't need to send for Daniel so often on the pretext of wanting to change his will, would he? Charlotte reasoned inwardly. She darted a brief look at Daniel but there was nothing in his face to suggest that he had even thought of pointing this out to her. She frowned a little. In his place, she would certainly have done so.

But then, she was *not* in his place, was she? she told herself. And if she had been no doubt she too could have afforded to be magnanimous... to allow her poor failure of an assistant to think she had scored a victory.

Suddenly she was as resentful of him for that magnanimity as she would have been had he pointed out the weakness in her argument.

At the top of the stairs the landing ran in both directions, and, as Charlotte turned instinctively to her right, Daniel touched her lightly on her arm.

'It's this way,' he told her, indicating the left-hand passage.

Immediately she turned round and then discovered that she was standing far too close to him. He didn't make any attempt to move, and she looked up at him, giving him an impatient querying glance.

'I've just realised how tiny you are,' he told her in answer to her unspoken question.

Immediately she was furiously indignant.

She had always hated people referring to her lack of height.

'I'm five-foot-three,' she told him fiercely.

She watched as his eyes crinkled as though he was trying to suppress his amusement.

No doubt he preferred tall women. Patricia Winters was tall, she remembered.

'I suppose that's why you wear those ridiculous shoes.'

Charlotte curled her fingers into her palms, her eyes flashing messages of anger and resentment.

'There is nothing ridiculous about my shoes,' she told him coldly. In point of fact, they were a pair of extremely expensive Charles Jourdan court shoes, the only pair she was ever likely to own for a very long time. And if her shoes were not ridiculous, well, the same could certainly not be said for her suit, she reflected miserably as, without waiting to see if Daniel was following her, she set off down the corridor.

Why, oh, why had she thrown out all her old clothes? They might have been dull, but they would certainly have been far more suited to her new role in life than what she was having to wear now.

Take the outfit she was wearing today. She hadn't realised until she had seen the brief lift of her mother's eyebrows this morning at breakfast just how dramatic the effect was of her short neat skirt worn with its matching long-line lean-fitting jacket. The fabric was a soft matt black wool crêpe and the jacket was lined in silk. Teamed with her cream silk shirt it was supposed to look crisply businesslike, but her mother had commented drily that she was rather glad that her father had retired before such fashions had reached the high-street bank of which he had been manager.

'That's nothing,' her father had chuckled. 'You should have seen the skirts they wore in the sixties. We had to replace all the filing cabinets because every time the girls reached into the top drawers of the existing ones you could see their——'

'That's enough, George,' had been her mother's firm denial of these reminiscences.

The corridor floor was covered in an oilcloth-type covering, no doubt for ease of cleaning, and when she heard Daniel's footsteps slowing down behind her Charlotte hesitated and then turned round.

He had stopped outside one of the doors and was knocking on it. As she went back to join him he was opening the door.

'Hello, John,' she heard him saying. 'I've brought you an extra visitor today.'

He was stepping back so that she could precede him into the room. It was a comfortable size, with a fireplace, and a very effective gas fire burning in the grate.

Either side of the fire were a pair of armchairs, and the bed, which was against one of the walls, had a wheelchair beside it.

The man seated in it was white-haired, his face leathery with age, the knuckles on his hands twisted with arthritis.

'Hmm... Well, she's pretty enough, at any rate,' John Balfour commented drily as he studied Charlotte. 'The new girlfriend, is she?'

Although she was embarrassed by his assumption that she was Daniel's girlfriend, Charlotte was not offended by his manner. She had had to deal with enough male clients of his generation over the years to accept that they were not being deliberately offensive, and indeed that they often thought they were being flattering and gallant.

'No, Charlotte is my new assistant, John. She's a *qualified* solicitor.'

'A solicitor, is she? Mmm... Well, she don't look much like Lydia.'

From the way he said it, Charlotte guessed that Lydia Jefferson was the yardstick against which he must measure any member of her sex who followed the same profession.

'Not physically, no, but there *are* certain similarities,' Daniel told him, much to Charlotte's surprise.

'Charlotte has had to miss out on her lunch to come here with me, so I suggest that you ring that bell of yours and order her a cup of tea.'

John Balfour grumbled that it was his room and not Daniel's and that he was perfectly capable of ordering tea for them all, without having to be told to do so.

'I should make you take it off what you'll be charging me for making out my new will,' he complained as he rang the bell beside the bed, but Charlotte could see that beneath his bluster he was pleased to have the excuse to prolong their visit.

Daniel was certainly in no hurry to get down to business. He talked easily to John Balfour about some new plans for altering the centre of the town, refusing to be drawn into an argument when the old man told him that the planners were ruining the place, complaining that they were making it unfit for anyone to live in.

'I see you're still driving Lydia's car,' he commented as he glanced out of the window. 'She was a fine woman, your great-aunt. Not a patch on her, your father. And as for you... Not getting too big for your boots, are you, now that you've had all this fuss made of you in the papers?'

'I hope not, John,' was Daniel's equable reply.

When a young girl came in, pushing a trolley with not only a pot of tea but also a plate of sandwiches and some cake, Daniel immediately got up to help her, and Charlotte noticed the way the girl flushed and then smiled at him.

'Thank God you didn't let her pour the tea. She'd have had it all over the place,' John commented once she had gone, and then he demanded sharply, 'Not still seeing the Winters widow, are you?' betraying the fact that he had not really believed that she, Charlotte, was Daniel's girlfriend at all.

'Paul Winters was a client of mine,' Daniel told him as he poured the tea.

'The woman is a bloodsucker. She got her claws well and truly into old Paul. I hear she got everything and that Gordon was left right out in the cold.'

'Gordon was only Paul's stepson,' Daniel said quietly. 'He has no legal claim on the estate.'

'No, but he was as close to Paul as a son would have been—closer. He did everything for him before she came along. A woman of twenty-three marrying a man of his age...'

'It does happen.'

'Yes, and we all know why.'

Daniel's mouth tensed, and Charlotte darted an anxious glance at John Balfour. He was obviously the kind of person who enjoyed stirring up trouble and inviting confrontation, but he must know how little Daniel would relish hearing him criticise Patricia, especially in front of a third party. Especially in front of her.

'This house seems very old,' she broke in quickly, avoiding looking directly at Daniel as she tried to redirect the conversation, not knowing why she should feel this need to change the subject. She had always disliked arguments, she told herself uncomfortably. It had nothing to do with any kind of desire to protect Daniel from the older man's critical probing. After all, why should *she* want to protect *him*?

'It must have a fascinating history.'

The look John Balfour gave her was extremely sardonic.

'I wouldn't know. I'm eighty-three, not eight-hundred.'

'Stop baiting her, John,' Daniel told him. 'You know quite well what Charlotte meant. Yes, it does have an interesting history,' he told her with a smile. 'As a matter of fact, it used to belong to my aunt.'

'Until she gave it to the town to be used as a home for the infirm and needy,' John Balfour butted in.

'My great-aunt left the house to the town, it's true, but unfortunately they couldn't afford to maintain it, so they sold it to the charitable trust that now runs it. It was originally Lydia's parents' home. When she first started up in practice she quarrelled with her parents, who were opposed to what she was doing. She bought the town house with a legacy from her godmother. My grandfather predeceased his parents and so eventually the house came down to her.

'She said that she had been banned from entering it during her father's lifetime and she had no intentions of entering it after his death. It was let out on a lease for a long time, and then, as John said, she willed it to the town when she died.'

'She must have been a very remarkable woman,' Charlotte commented.

'Yes, she was,' Daniel agreed, and there was a faint sadness in his eyes as though he still missed her. 'She was a philanthropist in the true sense of the word and——'

'She was as stubborn as a mule,' John Balfour interrupted. 'Stubbornest woman I ever met.'

Daniel laughed. 'Well, yes, she could be that as well,' he agreed. 'A trait which you and she both shared, eh, John?'

The older man grimaced, but he didn't deny Daniel's gentle charge.

It took almost two hours to sort out the very minor changes he apparently wanted made in his will, and while she listened Charlotte marvelled not just at Daniel's patience with him but also at his tact.

When they had finished Charlotte stood up and walked over to the door. As she started to open it she heard John Balfour saying to Daniel, 'Are you sure she's a solicitor? You'd never have seen Lydia wearing a skirt like that.'

Charlotte could feel her skin starting to burn. Her fingers gripped the door-handle until her knuckles were white. She dared not turn round.

'It's the fashion, John,' Daniel told him, but Charlotte could tell from the sound of his voice that he was smiling.

Charlotte could barely bring herself to look at Daniel as they went downstairs, keeping her face averted from him, her agitation causing her heart to thump uncomfortably. She could feel the shaming mixture of despair and weakness she had suffered from so much lately bringing tears to the back of her throat. She'd never used to be emotional like this. She had always been proud of the way she could control herself. And yet now that control, that belief in herself, had gone, leaving her feeling over-sensitive and too emotional.

When Daniel stopped to have a few words with the home's matron she darted ahead of him, quickly removing a tissue from her bag and blowing her nose firmly.

She was tucking the tissue out of sight when he reached her side.

'What's wrong?' he asked her, a brief frown touching his forehead as she looked away from him.

'You weren't upset by what John said about your clothes, were you? You needn't be. In his way, I suspect that he was actually trying to pay you a compliment.'

'And of course if I don't want people to make those sort of comments I could always wear longer skirts...is that it?' Charlotte challenged.

They were outside now and she felt sufficiently in control of herself to turn to face Daniel as they stood on the gravel driveway.

'Well, for your information, I *have* to wear these things. I don't have any other choice. *I* can't afford to replace them. That's what happens to people like me whose businesses fail. Not that you'd know about anything like that, or about any kind of failure, would you?' she demanded, her emotions finally getting the better of her self-control. 'Do you think I like people staring at me, wondering why on earth I'm wearing something so obviously unsuitable for my job?'

'Charlotte...' Daniel had taken hold of her arm, she realised, and he was pulling her gently but firmly towards him, bending towards her, his voice soothing and calm. 'My dear girl, there is nothing wrong with your clothes. In actual fact, and as a mere male, of course, I think that you ... that they look extremely attractive.'

As she stared at him he gave her a brief, almost apologetically boyish grin.

'Please don't take this the wrong way, but there *is* something about the sight of a woman wearing an attractively short skirt——'

'That is *exactly* what I mean,' Charlotte hissed at him, without letting him finish. '*That* kind of male chauvinism. You men are all the same. You all think that women dress with one goal in mind. Well, for your information, *I* dress to please myself and not ... to attract men.'

Even as she spoke Charlotte knew that it wasn't true. She had bought these clothes at Bevan's insistence, because she had wanted to please him.

She felt her throat clog with tears of misery and self-contempt.

'I'm sorry,' she heard Daniel saying. He was still holding on to her, but now the pressure of his fingers on her arm seemed to have changed, become caressing rather than restrictive.

She derided herself for the self-delusion of her imagination, pulling so abruptly away from him that he let her go.

He caught up with her just as she reached the car.

'Charlotte, *is* it true?' he asked her quietly. 'Can you really not afford——?'

Charlotte had endured enough. Why, oh, why had she allowed her temper to trap her into making that kind of admission?

'I don't want to discuss it,' she told him shortly.

As he unlocked the car door she thought she heard him saying grimly, 'Again... Is there anything else you don't want to discuss?'

But she decided that it was far wiser to ignore his question than to risk further self-betrayal by answering it.

CHAPTER FIVE

'You haven't forgotten about tonight, have you?'

Charlotte grimaced into the receiver as she listened to Sarah's question. 'No, I haven't. Dinner tonight at that new Italian place.'

'That's right. I'll be round about seven-thirty, and don't forget you're wearing the bandage.'

Charlotte groaned and then laughed.

'Charlotte, do you have the Higham file?'

She covered the receiver as she picked the file up off her desk and then handed it to Daniel.

'Look, I must go. See you tonight,' she told her sister, and then quickly replaced the receiver.

She had felt miserably uncomfortable with Daniel ever since her outburst outside the home. What on earth had possessed her to make that idiotic statement about not being able to afford to replace her clothes? The last thing she wanted was his pity, and yet she had practically invited it.

If it weren't for Daniel she could have settled down quite happily in her new job—very happily, in fact—but all the time she was conscious of his lack of trust in her. It was like having something rubbing against her skin, making her feel sore and irritable.

She was having lunch with Ginny and she was glad to get out into the sunshine with her when one o'clock finally arrived.

They had lunch in a small wine-bar several streets away, and Charlotte watched with wry amusement as the young clerks from the bank opposite ogled Ginny, until she realised that she was being surveyed by just as appraising, but rather more discreet looks by the man sitting on his own several tables away. Ignoring him, she concentrated on her lunch.

Ginny was chattering happily about her plans for the weekend.

'Poor Mr Jefferson,' she giggled. 'Mrs Winters rang this morning. She's coming in to see him this afternoon.'

'Perhaps he wants to see her,' Charlotte responded.

'Not a chance,' Ginny assured her. 'She's not his type. I'll bet he wouldn't want to see her at all if it weren't for——'

She broke off and flushed guiltily, and Charlotte was immediately aware that Ginny had thought better of whatever it was she had been about to say. She didn't press her to continue. If there was something about Daniel's relationship with Patricia Winters that she wasn't permitted to know then that was fine by her.

Ginny did not mention either Daniel or Patricia again but Charlotte's pleasure in her lunch had gone, and as they walked back to the office together she wondered why it was she found the thought of a personal relationship between Daniel and Patricia Winters so upsetting. After all, why should she be in the least concerned about Daniel's private life?

When she walked back into her office the communicating door was half open. She could hear voices from Daniel's office and she was just about to close the door when she heard her own name. She immediately stood still, knowing that she should walk away, but unable to stop herself from listening.

'But why is she your personal assistant, Daniel? You prefer to work alone. I've heard you say so, and yet suddenly you've taken on this...this...woman—and why a woman...why not a man?'

Charlotte held her breath; her nails were digging into the palms of her hands. She could feel the tension in all her muscles as she waited for Daniel's reply.

'I wasn't responsible for hiring her, Patricia,' she heard him saying. 'Richard interviewed her. He...we both felt that the work-load had become too heavy for us to give enough time to our clients.'

'Yes, but she is *your* assistant. She is working directly for you, on your cases,' Patricia Winters persisted.

It seemed to Charlotte as she stood listening that it was a long time before Daniel answered.

'Yes,' he agreed eventually. 'I felt that it would be wise initially if she was to work in collaboration with me rather than independently.'

'You mean she isn't up to the job. So why did Richard take her on? It isn't as though she's *that* attractive,' Patricia said dismissively.

'She's extremely well qualified,' Daniel responded.

'Yes,' Patricia agreed jeeringly. 'So well qualified that you have to supervise her work. Well, I'll tell

you this, Daniel . . . I don't want her involved in my
affairs.'

Their voices faded slightly and Charlotte guessed
that they were walking towards Daniel's office door.

She waited until she heard it open and she was
sure they were both safely outside in the corridor
before closing the communicating door and then
leaning against it while her body shook with chagrin
and rage.

So she had been right all along. He *didn't* trust
her, and those brief moments, those small conver-
sations over the last few days, when she had wondered if Sarah was right and if she had allowed
herself to misjudge the situation, had merely been
self-delusion.

She hated him . . . hated him . . . but nothing like
as much as she hated herself. She ached to go into
his office and tell him what he could do with his
job, but how could she?

Although she was loath to admit it to herself,
beneath her anger ran a contrary and extremely
dangerous emotion that came close to a feeling of
rejection, of hurt almost—the kind of emotion a
woman felt when a man to whom she was attracted
didn't want her.

What was *wrong* with her? she asked herself
crossly. Of course she wasn't attracted to him. How
could she be when she knew what he thought of
her?

Her pride would not allow her to be attracted to
a man who plainly thought so little of her.

And yet she couldn't help remembering a little
forlornly the compassion and kindness she had seen

him display to people like John Balfour. But then, the John Balfours of this world had not proved themselves to be inept and incompetent.

She would much rather he were honest with her instead of cloaking his feelings with smiles and a pseudo-friendly manner, because sometimes when they were working together, when he looked at her and smiled at her, she forget her antagonism and resentment of him and instead found herself being drawn to him, almost wanting to bask in the warmth of his approval and admiration. But that kind of weakness was something she wasn't going to give in to any more.

She had virtually heard him admit her own suspicions. What more evidence did she need?

She was glad when it was eventually time for her to leave for home. As she got into her car she told herself that it was ridiculous to feel so... so hurt by one man's opinion of her, especially when it only reinforced what she herself had already felt.

This afternoon after Patricia Winters had gone she had wanted to march into his office and confront him. To tell him that she herself was fully aware of her failure and that she had no need for him to underline it for her.

What was it she really wanted from him? she asked herself tiredly a couple of hours later as she got ready for her evening out with Sarah.

His understanding... his compassion... his kindness... his approval and professional admiration. Why? Why *should* his opinion have become so important to her and in such a short space of time?

She pushed the question away, almost afraid of confronting it.

'You're very quiet,' Sarah commented half an hour later as they drove towards the town. 'Is everything OK?'

'Yes, yes, fine,' Charlotte told her listlessly, but she could tell that her sister wasn't deceived.

'You aren't wearing the bandage,' Sarah accused her.

'No,' Charlotte agreed.

She had found another dress she had thought more suitable, a plain matt black jersey shift with a loose unstructured shape that was both elegant and flattering, and best of all was just that little bit longer than most of her other things.

'Mm...well, I must admit, I do like what you've got on,' Sarah told her.

Sarah, who had eaten at the new Italian restaurant before, directed Charlotte through the town, and Charlotte parked on a piece of waste ground opposite the restaurant.

It was rather more luxurious inside than she had expected, a full-blown restaurant, in fact, rather than a more simple trattoria.

They were shown first to the bar, and handed menus to study while they ordered their aperitifs.

Most of the other diners were couples, with the odd sprinkling of what looked like businessmen.

Once they had given their order they were shown almost immediately to their table.

'Not quite what I had expected,' Charlotte commented to her sister as she sat down.

Sarah pulled a face at her. 'Tony brought me here for our wedding anniversary treat, and I thought you'd enjoy it. I know how much you've always loved Italian food.'

They had just been served with their first course when Sarah suddenly leaned across the table and said softly, 'Don't turn round now, but I'm sure that your boss has just come in.'

'My boss?' Charlotte almost dropped her fork. 'You mean Daniel Jefferson?'

'The very same. At least, it looks like him. There's a woman with him. Tall ... and a bit hard-looking. Dark hair. They're sitting down at a table in the alcove. I think you can look now.'

Charlotte told herself that she wasn't going to look, that she wasn't in the least interested whether or not it was Daniel, but she couldn't stop herself from taking a quick glance into the alcove. Her heart started to thump unsteadily as she saw that Daniel was looking straight back at her.

She turned round quickly, and then to her consternation she heard Sarah saying, 'I think he must have seen you. It looks as though he's coming over.'

This time she didn't turn round, but she still knew the exact moment when Daniel reached their table. She could feel the tiny hairs at the back of her neck prickling slightly with tension as though her body had developed some special extra sense which recognised his presence.

'Charlotte, I thought it was you.'

Grimly Charlotte introduced him to her sister, gritting her teeth as Sarah openly flirted a little with him, telling him that she had seen him on television.

'I'd ask you to join us,' he told them both, 'but Patricia wants to discuss some business matters with me.'

Charlotte couldn't help it. She gave him a cynical disbelieving look that made him frown slightly as though he was about to say something but had thought better of it.

'Whew!' Sarah commented when he had gone. 'Now *that's* what I call a man. I can almost feel the steam coming out of my ears. Talk about sexy. I didn't think much of his partner, though. She was glaring daggers at you while he was over here. *He* might think they're having a business meeting, but I doubt that's what she thinks. You only have to look at the dress she's wearing. If the neckline was any lower it would be indecent.'

She frowned and stopped speaking as she saw the way that Charlotte was playing with her food. 'Char, what is it, what's wrong?'

'Nothing,' Charlotte told her, but they both knew she was lying. Charlotte felt miserably guilty. She knew that Sarah had wanted to give her a treat to cheer her up, and here she was, behaving like a sulky child.

'I'm sorry, Sarah,' she apologised to her sister, forcing her mouth into a smile. 'It's just...well, he knew I was coming here tonight. He walked into my office while we were on the phone. Why did he have to bring her here? It's almost as though...'

'As though what?' Sarah questioned her, her expression suddenly softening as she leaned across the table and took hold of one of Charlotte's hands.

'Do you know what I think?' she told her gently.
'I think you're beginning to fall in love with him.'

Immediately Charlotte snatched her hand away.
'Don't be ridiculous. I barely know him.'

'Since when did time have anything to do with
it? I fell in love with Tony within seconds of meeting
him. When he reversed into my car I was so furious,
and then when he got out of his car and came over
to apologise to me I took one look at him and suddenly I wouldn't have cared if he'd wrecked my car
completely.'

'*That* was different,' Charlotte told her sister
miserably. 'Tony shared your feelings.'

'Ah ha, so you *do* admit that you feel something
for him?' Sarah pounced, and then immediately
apologised as she saw Charlotte's expression.

'I don't know what I feel any more,' Charlotte
told her wretchedly. 'I only know I wish I'd never
met him. Sarah... he doesn't trust me, never mind
anything else. He thinks I'm a failure and he's right.
I——'

'It didn't look to me like he thought you were a
failure when he came over to talk to us just now,'
Sarah interrupted her wryly.

'To talk to *us*.' Charlotte grimaced. '*You* were
the one he was talking to, not me.'

'Mm, but *you* were the one he was watching.'

'Look, I don't want to talk about it. Can we
please change the subject?'

'If that's what you want. What would you like
to talk about? Dad has very high hopes of taking
the best rose prize in the local show this summer,'
she told Charlotte with a straight face. 'Personally

I think he could have a lot of competition. Old Mr Thorneycroft——'

'All right, all right,' Charlotte interrupted her, 'but it's pointless talking about Daniel, Sarah. It's useless, a hopeless mess.' She gave her sister a wistful smile. 'I know you mean well, but talking about it won't do any good. The best thing for me to do is to stop thinking about him, not keep focusing my mind on him.'

For the rest of the meal they chatted in a comfortable familiar way about family matters, Sarah's children, and their own childhood, but Charlotte had little appetite for the marvellous food, pushing it around her plate, much to the distress of their waiter.

From the moment she had seen Daniel with Patricia all she had wanted to do was disappear, but pride kept her at their table. She wasn't going to let him see just how much of an effect he had on her.

Even so, she was relieved when Sarah finished her final cup of *cappucino* and announced that it was probably time they left.

Outside it had gone rather cool, and Charlotte was glad they didn't have very far to walk to the car, since she hadn't brought a coat with her.

She unlocked the doors and they both got in, but, when she turned the key in the ignition after a few uncertain coughs, the engine refused to fire.

'What is it? What's wrong?' Sarah asked her anxiously.

'I don't know,' Charlotte admitted, and then as she glanced briefly at the indicator panels her heart sank.

'I've run out of petrol,' she told her sister hollowly.

'What? Oh, no! The nearest all-night service station is the one on the bypass, and that's a two-mile walk.'

'Yes, I know. Look, you stay here,' Charlotte told her. 'I'll go and——'

'You'll do no such thing. A woman walking along a main road on her own at this time of night just isn't safe. We could always ring Mum and Dad.'

Charlotte shook her head. 'It would take them longer to get here than it would for us to walk to the garage and back.'

Charlotte started to get out of the car, shivering as the cold wind cut straight through her dress.

She didn't even have a petrol can in the boot. Credit cards were something she had stopped using from the moment she had closed down her business, but fortunately she did have her cheque-book and her cheque card.

Of all the things to happen. Normally she was so meticulous about keeping her tank well filled with petrol, but she had worked late several evenings and the local garage had been closed, and somehow or other she had had so many other things on her mind that she had completely forgotten how low on petrol she actually was.

There were several cars parked with hers on the waste ground, presumably belonging to the other diners, and as she turned round Charlotte froze.

Two people were crossing the road and heading for the waste ground. She recognised them immediately. Patricia Winters was walking very close to Daniel, her hand holding his arm as she spoke to him.

At first Charlotte thought that he hadn't seen her, but suddenly he stopped and, disengaging himself from Patricia's grip, came across to them.

'Is everything all right?' he asked.

Charlotte's immediate instinctive response was to deny what had happened, but Sarah was too quick for her, telling Daniel wryly, 'We seem to have run out of petrol.'

'It's all right. I was just about to walk to the service station to get some,' Charlotte said quickly, immediately aware of the way Daniel was frowning as he focused on her.

'You can't do that,' he told her firmly. 'It's far too dangerous. Look, why don't I give you both a lift? It would seem the sensible thing to do. I think your car will be quite safe here, Charlotte, if you lock it up.'

'There's no need for that,' Charlotte started to say, but once again Sarah overruled her, smiling at Daniel as she said warmly,

'Thank you. That's very kind of you.'

With both Daniel and Sarah standing there watching her, Charlotte had no option but to lock the car and walk with Daniel across to where he was parked.

He wasn't driving his great-aunt's car this time, but a small Mercedes saloon.

Charlotte could see from the look on Patricia Winters's face how furious she was.

'How on earth could anyone be stupid enough to run out of petrol?' she demanded when Daniel explained what had happened.

'Quite easily,' Daniel told her mildly. 'I've done it myself. Look, let's get in the car, it's cold out here,' he added, unlocking it, and moving slightly towards Charlotte as he opened the door, so that his body protected hers from the cold wind.

He hadn't done it deliberately, of course, he had simply been opening the car door, but nevertheless for those few seconds when she was mercifully protected from the cold she felt bathed in a warmth as treacherously emotional as it was physical.

Daniel was asking Sarah exactly where they wanted dropping off, and when she told him he said, 'I'll drop you off first, then, Patricia, since your place is closer.'

In the darkness of the rear seat of the Mercedes, Sarah reached for Charlotte's hand and gave it a brief squeeze, and Charlotte could tell from the angry set of Patricia Winters's head that she was far from pleased by Daniel's suggestion.

As Charlotte had expected, Patricia's house was extremely large, its façade floodlit by security lights as they drove up.

'I hope you at least intend to see me to the door,' she told Daniel in extremely acid tones as he stopped the car.

'Of course,' he agreed cordially, and while Charlotte and Sarah waited he paused to have several seconds' conversation with her before she disappeared inside.

'Well, there's someone who isn't at all pleased by the way the evening's turned out,' Sarah commented to Charlotte as they waited for Daniel to rejoin them.

It was only another few miles to Charlotte's parents' house, but to Charlotte the journey seemed to last forever. She discovered when the Mercedes finally stopped in her parents' drive that she had been tightening her muscles so much that they actually physically ached.

It was left to Sarah to thank Daniel for his kindness. Charlotte could barely bring herself to look at him, never mind anything else. What a complete idiot he must think her, despite his comment about anyone being able to run out of petrol. It was such a stupid thing to have done, but what frightened her most of all was how much it showed the way her concentration had lapsed. What if she made a similar mistake with her work? What if she forgot or overlooked something important?

She gave a tense shudder, causing Daniel to tell her almost roughly, 'You're cold. You should have a coat. Oh, and don't worry about getting into work on time in the morning if you're delayed with your car.'

'You didn't even thank him,' Sarah rebuked Charlotte mildly once they were inside, 'and he was so kind.'

Charlotte gave her a wan smile.

'And what's all this about his not liking or trusting you?' she added. 'It seemed to me that he was extremely concerned about you, going to all that trouble. It was obvious that Patricia Winters wasn't at all pleased to have their evening cut short by our presence.'

'He's just that kind of man,' Charlotte told her listlessly. 'It means nothing.'

Sarah's eyebrows rose.

'Really? When you shivered I thought for a moment he was actually going to take off his jacket and wrap it round you.'

Charlotte flushed and moved uncomfortably from one foot to the other. 'Don't be silly. You always did have an over-vivid imagination.'

'You think so? I think you're wallowing so deeply in your self-inflicted sea of self-pity that you don't want to see the truth.'

'So he was polite,' Charlotte responded angrily. 'So what? As I've just told you, that's the kind of man he is.'

'If you say so,' Sarah told her, but Charlotte could see that she wasn't convinced.

'Pity I was with you,' Sarah mused. 'Otherwise he could have had you all to himself, and then——'

'Sarah, please. *Don't* . . .'

The anguish in Charlotte's voice caused Sarah to stop and look gravely at her sister. 'I'm sorry. I didn't mean . . . You *are* in love with him, aren't you?'

'No. No, of course I'm not,' Charlotte denied, but the words sounded unsure and unconvincing even to her own ears.

Long after she should have been asleep she was lying awake, trying to come to terms with the intensity of her own emotions.

How could she have fallen in love with Daniel? It was impossible, idiotic . . . inevitable.

She buried her face in her pillow, trying to stifle the sharp moan of protest that rose in her.

She *couldn't* love him. She *must* not love him. But as she lay there, her eyes hot and dry with the tears she refused to shed, she knew that she did.

CHAPTER SIX

DANIEL didn't trust her judgement, Charlotte knew that, and yet as the days passed she began to wonder if Sarah had been right and if she had allowed the doubts and lack of self-confidence brought on by the failure of her practice to affect her, because increasingly Daniel *was* asking her opinion on various aspects of his cases, including her in interviews with his clients both at the office and when he had to go out on client visits. He had even praised her for the work she had done on constructing a case for one of those clients, telling her that she had picked up on a very important aspect of the case which had eluded him.

It became a familiar thing to Charlotte to have him standing beside her desk, his hands resting either side of her on the edge of it as he leaned forward to see what she was doing, and, where initially she had seen his presence as watchful distrust, she was now beginning to view it more in the light of a genuine acceptance of the validity of the points she was making.

One afternoon, when she had been enthusiastically describing to him a little-known precedent which she felt sure would strengthen a case that had previously seemed very uncertain, he had suddenly reached out and very gently tucked her hair behind her ear, saying softly, 'So much passion. I almost wish——'

Exactly what he had wished he had never told her because Anne had come hurrying into his office to tell him that a client had unexpectedly turned up in Reception, and Daniel had still been with him when Charlotte had eventually left for home.

'You're looking a lot more cheerful,' Sarah commented at the weekend. She had come round with the children, who were outside in the garden ostensibly helping their grandfather, while Sarah, Charlotte and their mother prepared lunch.

'It wouldn't have anything to do with a certain oh, so sexy solicitor we both know, would it?'

Charlotte laughed but refused to be drawn. Her feelings were still too new and tender to be discussed with anyone else, and, besides, Daniel had neither said nor done anything to indicate that she had the same effect on him as he did on her. That was if you discounted the way he sometimes smiled at her and the tenderness in his fingers the other afternoon when they had brushed against her skin.

Dreamily Charlotte wondered why it was that the lightest touch from one man could have a far more devastating effect on a woman's senses than the most intense display of passion from another.

Daniel had aroused her more quickly, more intensely, and certainly far more unexpectedly with that one small touch than had Bevan's most passionate kisses.

She squirmed a little uncomfortably at the direction of her own thoughts. It was useless to try to deny to herself that she was beginning to spend far too much time daydreaming about what it might be like if Daniel were to kiss her with passion and desire when just the touch of his fingers had such an electric effect on her.

She could still recall the sharp spine-tingling sensation she had felt, the shock of knowing that her whole body was reacting to him, and reacting not just with pleasure, but intense desire as well, the kind of desire in fact that she could never remember experiencing before.

When *he* had touched her her whole body had been filled with a need, a yearning almost that had made her instinctively relax against him, virtually nestling her head against his shoulder. She flushed a little as she recalled how potentially betraying her behaviour must have been, but Daniel had not been in any hurry to withdraw from her, and the look in his eyes when they were interrupted had not been one that had suggested that he had welcomed that interruption.

It was a happy weekend, with Charlotte feeling more relaxed and at ease with herself and the rest of the world than she had felt in a long time. It was only when her mother commented after watching her play with Sarah's children that it had been a long time since she had heard her laughing that she appreciated the blight she had cast on other people's lives as well as her own.

'I'm sorry, Ma,' she apologised. 'I haven't been the easiest person to get along with lately, have I?'

'You've had good reason for feeling unhappy,' her mother told her gently.

On Monday morning, when she drove to work, Charlotte was not only feeling happily content, she was actually looking forward to being at work as well. And not just because she was now finding her feet and enjoying the actual work. Even the clothes which had caused her such irritated despair no longer seemed quite as out of place as they had done, and when, after she had parked her car and was walking to the office, a workman whistled at her, instead of resenting it she turned round and gave him a brief grin, amused to notice that he actually blushed while his workmates teased him.

'My goodness, you're chirpy this morning,' Anne commented when she saw her.

'Did *you* have a good weekend?' Charlotte asked her.

Anne groaned. 'No. Junior here is kicking as though he's got four legs and not two, and my husband complained that I kept him awake all last night. It was almost a relief to get in to work this morning.'

Charlotte smiled sympathetically. Anne did look tired and her pregnancy was well advanced now.

'I wish some of this good humour would rub off on me,' she added. 'I saw Daniel a few minutes ago and he was full of the joys of spring as well... Is it something the two of you put in your coffee?' she asked wryly.

Anne drank tea because of the baby, and Charlotte laughed dutifully but ducked her head a little so that her hair swung forward against her face, hiding the colour she could feel warming her skin.

Daniel had a busy morning with several appointments, and then just before lunch he came into Charlotte's office to tell her that one of his cases had unexpectedly been brought forward and that he would be in court for the rest of the day.

She had been checking on something when he had walked in, and as she looked at him the way he studied her made her flush slightly. There was a fluttery feeling inside her stomach, she felt slightly light-headed, dizzy almost, and at the same time so happy that she could feel her mouth starting to curl into a warm smile.

'I had hoped we might have lunch together today,' Daniel told her, and then as her heart started to leap with excitement he added, 'There are a couple of cases I wanted to discuss with you with the trials coming up soon and we never seem to get time here.' He glanced at his watch. 'Unfortunately there just isn't going to be time.'

Charlotte nodded, unable to trust herself to speak.

'You *are* happy here, aren't you, Charlotte?' he asked her unexpectedly.

She nodded again.

'Good. Because I shouldn't want to lose you.'

Charlotte looked at him, her expression unguarded and vulnerable.

'You're a very valuable asset to the firm,' he told her while her colour came and went. She was too stunned by the extraordinary unexpectedness of his praise to think of anything to say.

For a long time after he had gone, she could do nothing other than sink down into her chair and stare blindly at the wall while his words echoed and re-echoed through her mind.

He didn't want to lose her. He thought her a valuable asset. Her chest grew tight with the bubbles of euphoria building up inside it. Suddenly she felt as though there was nothing she could not do, no goal she could not achieve. She daydreamed through the afternoon on a crest of dazed happiness, only to realise at half-past four that she had achieved virtually nothing all afternoon.

Some asset you are, she told herself as she forced her attention back to her work, pausing only to telephone her mother and tell her that she was going to be working late.

She barely noticed the others leaving as she concentrated on the work in front of her, but every now and again her hand would falter as she wrote her notes, and she would start staring into space, thinking about Daniel...remembering what he had said.

At half-past seven she flexed her tense fingers and went to make herself a cup of coffee. Another half an hour should see it through.

She sat down at her desk, frowning as she studied what she had written. It was a complex case and one that required a great deal of research. There wasn't a lot more she could do this evening. She sipped her coffee and sat back in her chair, a tender smile curling her mouth.

She closed her eyes, remembering how often recently she had sat like this with Daniel standing behind her.

'Charlotte, you're working late.'

Her eyes flew open as Daniel walked into the room, dropping his case on the floor and removing his coat, which he threw on to a chair.

As he loosened his tie slightly he told her, 'The Ipsom case has been put back. The one before it proved more troublesome than expected. That's a whole afternoon hanging around the court... What is it you're working on?' he asked her, coming to stand behind her in the way she had just been secretly remembering.

She could feel the heat singing down her spine as he stood there, her body deliciously—shockingly, really—aware of him and the pleasure that knowing he was so close to her gave her.

He grimaced when he saw the name on the file. 'There's no doubt about it that there was gross negligence on the part of the employer, but I can't see how we're going to prove it. The man worked alone, there were no witnesses, and the employers claim that he had a history of not using the guards properly so that he was in fact responsible for his own injuries.'

'Mm, I know,' she agreed. 'Our client claims that it was standing working practice to use the machines without their guards.'

'Yes, but we can't prove that.'

'He mentions in his statement that this practice had been in use for a very long time, that the man he took over from had warned him about it.'

'Yes, but he has since died and so we can't use him as a witness,' he said wryly.

'No, but if he sustained any injuries at work they would be on his medical records... If his death only occurred fairly recently, those records should still be available.'

'That's rather a lot of ifs,' Daniel told her, 'but you're right. It *is* worth investigating.'

'I think so,' Charlotte told him excitedly. 'Because if we can prove——'

She stopped suddenly.

Daniel was looking at her in a way that made her forget all about her work.

Her eyes grew wide and dark as his glance drifted across her face, his glance holding hers for several heartbeats of time before his attention focused on her mouth.

She could feel her heart racing, a frantic fast thud that made her feel breathless and giddy. 'I've been thinking about you all afternoon... about this,' he told her simply, and then he lowered his head and started to kiss her gently, caressing her mouth with his, and then when she had made no effort to repulse him he drew her slowly to her feet, one hand warm and firm against her spine, while the fingers of the other pushed gently into her hair, easing it back off her face.

'Your hair feels like silk,' he whispered against her mouth. 'Do you know that?'

He kissed her again, more deeply this time.

'Hold me, Charlotte,' he begged her. 'Put your arms around me and hold me...'

She obeyed him without even thinking about hesitating, making a small female sound of pleasure in her throat at the sensual contact of his body against her own.

He was stroking her back now, moulding her against him as he kissed her. She was starting to tremble, to shiver with the intensity of her body's arousal.

Suddenly they weren't kissing gently any longer, and Charlotte opened her mouth, wanting the intimate thrust of his tongue against her own, clinging to him, her nails digging into him as he responded to her invitation.

She could feel him moving back from her, and wasn't sure what he was doing until she opened her eyes and realised that he was shrugging off his jacket, letting it fall to the floor while he held on to her and kept on kissing her with increasing passion.

The sensation of his body against hers with only his shirt and her silk blouse and bra between them sent her nerve-endings into a delirium. He urged her closely against him, whispering to her that he wanted to feel her hands on his skin, that he wanted to touch her... to taste her. He kissed her throat and the small exposed V of flesh at the opening of her shirt, and all the time she clung to him, responding to him almost feverishly, achingly aware of how much she longed for the touch of his hands on her bare skin...how much she longed to be able to touch him in the same way.

He kissed her mouth again, biting gently and then less gently at her bottom lip while she trembled and whimpered with desire.

Much more of this and she would be begging him to remove both her clothes and his own, something that Bevan had never aroused her to do even once in their relationship.

She felt his hand against her breast, his thumb rubbing softly against the silk that separated her from his touch. Her nipples, already hard, pulsed with fierce desire. Already she could almost feel what it would be like if he kissed them, suckled at them... She shuddered wildly, clinging to him.

Outside in the street a car backfired, and instantly both of them tensed. Charlotte opened her eyes and found that Daniel was looking into them.

He lifted his hand from her breast, to smooth the tousled hair from her face, his fingertips blessedly cool against her hot skin.

'This isn't really the time or the place, is it?' he said thickly.

He was still holding her, and she could feel his physical arousal. The knowledge that he wanted her made her own body pulse and ache, but when he started to ease himself gently away from her she made no move to stop him.

His hands cupped her face, framing it as he bent his head and kissed first one corner of her mouth and then the other, and then with a small groan he touched his tongue-tip to her top lip and then slowly parted it from her bottom one, his mouth just a breath away from hers.

'If I start kissing you again now I'm never going to be able to stop,' he told her huskily. 'I've got a meeting this evening that I just can't get out of. Have dinner with me tomorrow night, Charlotte.'

She nodded, not trusting herself to speak.

He kissed her gently, and then again fiercely, pulling her abruptly against him so that she could feel the intimacy of his arousal before releasing her and standing back from her.

'I daren't stay here any longer with you,' he told her.

'I was just about to leave.' Her voice was jerky and husky. Charlotte dared not look at him. She was too afraid that if she did she would start pleading with him to stay, to finish what he had started. The intensity of her own desire confused her. She had never felt like this before. Never experienced such need, such immediacy. The shock of it left her feeling bemused, unable to function properly.

'I'll see you to your car,' Daniel told her, but as they walked across the empty square together they kept their distance from one another, as though they were both afraid that if they got too close they would be overwhelmed by the same explosive need which had engulfed them in the office.

As she drove home Charlotte tried to analyse logically what had happened, but it was impossible. Tomorrow night she was having dinner with him... She shivered as she remembered how she had felt when he had touched her... when he had kissed her... If something so small as a kiss could affect her like that, what was going to happen to her if he made love to her...?

'I shan't be in for supper tonight,' Charlotte told her mother as casually as she could over breakfast. 'I'm having dinner with... with Daniel.'

She tried hard to say his name with cool indifference, as though having dinner with him were something of little importance, but she knew that her mother wasn't deceived. Her voice cracked a little and became betrayingly husky, and she knew that beneath her discreet covering of make-up she was flushing as guiltily as a schoolgirl.

But tactfully her mother made no comment other than to ask her if she was coming home to change first or if they were going out straight from the office...

Charlotte told her that she wasn't sure. She hoped that she would be able to come home first. She would have liked to have had the opportunity to change into something other than her office suits—the black dress she had worn to have dinner with Sarah perhaps—and it would be nice to be able to wash her hair as well, and to shower, perhaps using that ridiculously expensive body lotion which Sarah and Tony had given her for Christmas.

She trembled a little, well aware of the dangerous paths her thoughts were taking.

When was the last time she had thought about preparing for a date with so much awareness of where it might lead? When had she *ever* prepared for a date knowing that already she was imagining the man concerned as a lover?

In her university days there had been a fellow student with whom she had believed herself in love, and they had been lovers, but she had not felt with him one-tenth of the intensity she had experienced in Daniel's arms last night. And yet the heady sexual experiences of one's youth—one's first sexual experiences—she had read somewhere were the yardstick with which to measure other sexual experiences for the rest of one's life.

Her body trembled again. She had never looked forward to sharing the intimate experience of sex with a man with so much almost wanton mental pleasure, nor had she ever imagined herself doing so.

Last night she had lain awake, her mind filled by feverish imaginings of the touch of Daniel's hands, his mouth . . . of the scent and the taste of his body, of all the ways she wanted to love him and be loved by him, and that had been a totally new experience for her.

She and Bevan had discussed, calmly and logically, the impossibility of fitting a sexual relationship into their busy lives, and had just as easily and calmly decided to shelve it until their busy schedules permitted them to take time off together to develop that side of their relationship.

'We'll hire a French château and spend every evening making love in front of a huge log fire,' Bevan had told her dramatically, and yet her pulse-rate hadn't lifted one single beat at the images he had drawn for her, while merely remembering the way Daniel had looked at her, never mind touched her, set off such a fierce surge of physical responsiveness inside her that she had to compress her muscles against it.

It was a bewildering, exhilarating sensation, this discovery that she was so totally physically, mentally and emotionally responsive to Daniel.

And he must feel something for her, otherwise he would not have said the things he had said...done the things he had done.

Her heart sang as she drove to work, and even though she knew that Daniel would be in court for most of the day her heart still gave a giddy skip of excitement and elation as she stepped into the building.

Tonight she would be with him. Tonight... But it was hours away.... As she walked into her office she looked regretfully at the closed communicating door, and then, on an impulse she could not resist, she opened it and walked through into Daniel's office.

His desk was clear and empty. She touched it, rimming the leather-covered blotter with her fingertip and then stroking the top of his chair.

She closed her eyes and breathed deeply, certain that beneath the smell of leather and polished wood she could just catch the faint scent of Daniel's soap, and then, as she opened her eyes, she derided herself for being over-imaginative, but her eyes still glowed with warmth and her lips were parted in a soft reminiscent smile as she remembered the warm male scent of his skin when he had kissed her and the way he had buried his mouth in her neck and whispered in her ear that he loved the silky feel of her hair.

A tiny convulsive shiver raced through her. The office door opened and she swung round, anticipation shining in her eyes, but it wasn't Daniel who was standing there, it was Patricia Winters.

'Oh,' she said curtly. 'Where's Daniel?' she demanded peremptorily.

Charlotte felt herself flush with irritation at her bad manners, but she reminded herself that the woman was a client and said as pleasantly as she could, 'He's in court today. Can I help you?'

The look Patricia gave her was as derogatory as was her drawled, 'I hardly think so,' and then she was sweeping out of the office in the same arrogant way in which she had swept in, leaving behind her the heavy scent of Poison.

An apt choice of perfume for her, Charlotte decided acidly after she had opened the windows to get rid of the smell.

Had she and Daniel ever been lovers, or was it simply, as Anne and Ginny had implied, that she had been chasing him, seeking to put their business relationship on a more intimate footing?

As she went back to her own office she chewed distractedly on her bottom lip. Everything she had learned about Daniel since she had worked for him told her that he was simply not the kind of man to do anything about which he was not completely sincere.

Far from being the publicity-hungry media-mad person she had first imagined, he had an integrity that even she had been forced to acknowledge.

She had recognised that integrity even while she had still been filled with bitter resentment against him, forced to acknowledge it even as she had railed against his crushing judgement of her own failure.

But now she had overcome that resentment, because he had begun to show that he must have changed his mind about her. He was beginning to trust her, professionally. He had even told her that he valued her as a colleague.

And he had also told her that he wanted her as a woman. Her stomach lurched and she breathed in deeply. From the window she could see Patricia crossing the road. When she reached the other pavement a man walking along it stopped to talk to her. He was tall and grey-haired and it was obvious from the expression on Patricia's face that he had said something flattering to her. They walked off together, the man listening attentively to whatever it was that Patricia was saying to him.

Charlotte turned her attention back to her desk. The last thing she felt like was work. What you need, my girl, is some self-discipline, she told herself severely. You're not here to sit daydreaming about Daniel.

But that was exactly what she *was* doing, she realised guiltily an hour later when her attention drifted away from her work for the third time to dwell dreamily on the way Daniel had touched her last night, the way he had held her... the way he had kissed her... If she just closed her eyes for a second she could almost recapture the sensation of his body against hers, his mouth...

She jumped guiltily as her telephone rang, picking up the receiver.

'Charlotte...'

She tensed as she heard Daniel's voice.

'Look, I haven't got much time. I just wanted to check that it was still on for this evening. It doesn't look as though I'm going to get back to the office, so I wondered if I could pick you up, say around seven-thirty. I've booked a table at a new place that's recently opened.'

'Yes, seven-thirty will be fine,' Charlotte managed to croak as he told her that he had to go and said a brief goodbye.

Fortunately the rest of the day was so busy that she didn't have time to indulge in any further day-dreaming, but then at five o'clock, just as she was about to leave, Richard came into her office to ask her if she was settling in all right and if she was happy.

She told him that she was, relieved when he said that he couldn't stop to chat because his wife had organised a dinner party with some friends, and it was only as she drove home that she recognised that, had Richard asked her the same question during her first week of working at the practice, she would have given him a very different answer indeed.

Perhaps Sarah *had* been right...perhaps she *had* been too full of self-pity, too ready to leap to the wrong conclusions—perhaps it was after all natural in the circumstances that initially at least Daniel should want to keep an eye on her, if only for the protection of his clients, she admitted fair-mindedly.

Perhaps she had been over-sensitive in feeling that he was condemning her, contrasting his success with her failure.

But she was still a little uncomfortably aware of that difference between them. She might no longer resent him, but, if she was honest, she did slightly envy him. Not so much his success, but his *ability* to succeed, the skills which had made it possible for him to succeed, skills which she evidently did not possess.

Stop it, she warned herself as she drove. Don't start spoiling things by dwelling on what's past.

It was a command which she repeated to herself as she prepared for their dinner date.

She had had her shower, carefully and to her mind rather self-indulgently smoothing her skin with scented body lotion. She found it rather hard to meet her own eyes in the mirror when she slid on the silk underwear which had been an impulse present to herself and which so far she had never worn. There was nothing particularly provocative about the very simple bra and brief set, that was if you discounted the way the silk felt and the way it clung to her skin.

Similarly the black dress was nowhere near as outwardly sexy as the Alaia number, but she felt far more comfortable in it, and that gave her a confidence she knew she would not have had had she been wearing the other dress.

She was upstairs when she heard his car pulling up outside. She looked quickly in the mirror, checking her appearance. Would he be as aware as she was of the heightened tension that made her skin glow and her pupils seem much larger than usual?

She looked at her mouth. Was she wearing too much lipstick? Would he look at her and know that when she had been applying the soft pink colour she had been remembering what it had felt like to have his mouth moving on hers? And that she had been anticipating how she would feel when he kissed her again?

She heard him ringing the doorbell, and her mother going to answer it, and knew it was time for her to go downstairs.

She had, of course, to introduce him to her parents, both of whom, she could tell, liked him immediately.

He was driving the Jaguar, and as he opened the passenger door for her she felt the happiness which had been bubbling inside her all day start to fizz into dizzy expectation.

'I haven't eaten at this new place before,' he told her as he started the car, 'but I've heard very good reports of it.'

'How far is it?' Charlotte asked him.

He told her, explaining that it had originally been an old farmhouse close to the river which had now been renovated and converted into a restaurant.

'We handled the conveyancing when the place was sold, and there were several complications with the change of use application; however, it was granted in the end.

'Carl trained with the Roux brothers. That's how he met Elise, his wife. They make a good team.'

To reach the restaurant they had to drive off the main road and down a narrow gravel lane.

The forecourt was well illuminated with security lights, and the same lights discreetly floodlit the front of the building.

It was very old, long and low, with small mullioned windows, and Charlotte could just make out the outlines of lawns and paths to the sides of

the building which, Daniel told her, led down to
the river, and a stone terrace at the rear of the
farmhouse which was used for lunch parties in the
summer.

As they walked towards the building Daniel
slipped his hand under her elbow to guide her across
the gravel car park.

Immediately and instinctively Charlotte moved
closer to him. It was as though her body was automatically seeking the warmth and comfort of his,
the *intimacy* of his, she reflected. Their footsteps
slowed a little as though both of them were silently
enjoying their physical intimacy, and then a car
drew up behind them and Charlotte moved slightly
away, quickening her walking pace a little.

As they reached the building she acknowledged
that all she really wanted this evening was simply
to be with Daniel, that if he turned to her now and
took her in his arms and whispered to her, 'Let's
forget about the meal,' she wouldn't have raised
one single objection. On the contrary.

She blinked a little as Daniel opened the door
and the silence was broken by the hum of voices
from inside.

She was glad to see that the renovations and the
décor had been kept very simple.

Someone, she recognised, had gone to a great
deal of trouble to create an atmosphere of auth-
enticity, allied to discreet modern comforts.

The building was obviously centrally heated, but
the radiators were hidden discreetly out of sight,
the exposed beams had been cleaned and limed, and
the plaster infills between them had been washed

in a soft pinky earthy colour which Charlotte suspected was a recreation of the original kind of wash that would have been used on a building of this age.

The stone-flagged floors were covered in rich, warmly hued rugs and the furniture was thankfully not of the dark oak tapestry-covered pseudo-Tudor type so beloved of a certain type of pub.

'What do you think?' Daniel asked her as they went into the bar area.

'I like it,' Charlotte told him. She smiled at him as she spoke, and then her smile faded as she saw the way he was looking back at her. At her eyes and then her mouth, making her feel as though her skin had become so sensitised that he had actually physically touched it.

Charlotte supposed later that they must have ordered drinks but she couldn't remember doing so—what she did know was that she certainly did not give the extensive and imaginative menu anything like the concentration it deserved.

By the time she and Daniel were shown to their table she couldn't have cared less what she ate.

Their conversation, outwardly mundane, for her was merely a cloak for what she was feeling, Charlotte acknowledged as she watched as Daniel spoke to her.

How was it that she had never realised before that even the most simple ordinary things about another human being could have such a profound and erotic effect on one's senses?

Just the way Daniel moved his hands, for instance... Just the way he smiled, the way he looked at her, the way his eyes looked into hers, the way he sat, the way he moved—everything about him affected her so powerfully that she could have sat for hours, totally absorbed in watching him.

As she listened to him she realised what a powerful effect his great-aunt had had on his life, almost envying her for the love he obviously had for her.

'It must be wonderful to have that kind of self-confidence,' Charlotte told him when he was describing to her how his great-aunt, after being refused a partnership by any local practice, had decided to set up on her own.

'Oh, I don't think it was so much that she had self-confidence. I think it was more a grim necessity. You see, she knew that if she didn't find some way to practise and to become totally independent from her parents she would be sucked back into the lifestyle they had planned for her.'

'Mm. It seems incredible these days to think of a woman, an adult woman, being so circumscribed.'

'Yes,' he agreed. 'We tend to forget how greatly life has changed for people this century, how many things we take for granted now that had never even been imagined at the time of the First World War. I hope you've left room for some pudding,' he added. 'The sweet trolley here is supposed to be something very special.'

Charlotte smiled at him. All she wanted now was to be alone with him, to be held in his arms. To be touched, kissed... She could feel the heat building inside her body, the need which was instantly recognisable even though she had never experienced it with such intensity before.

She closed her eyes, trying to control her feelings, and instantly had a mental image of the two of them together, moonlight silvering their entwined naked bodies, both of them lost to the passion their desire had created.

Immediately she opened her eyes, her face hot, her brain trying to grapple with the extraordinary intensity of her mental imaginings.

'I don't think I want any pudding,' she told him huskily. 'Just . . . just coffee.'

As she looked at him, she wondered if he could have guessed what was going through her mind, if he wanted her with the same intensity with which she wanted him.

So this was what loving someone did to you. Extraordinary that she had never guessed she could feel like this; that Bevan, whom she had quite happily planned to marry eventually, had never come anywhere near making her feel like this.

She sipped her coffee, watching Daniel buttering a biscuit. His fingers were long and lean, his movements deft. She remembered how she had felt when his thumb had rubbed slowly against her breast. Her coffee-cup rattled in its saucer as she replaced it.

Daniel looked up at her, his eyes darkening, the pupils dilating.

He pushed his plate away, the biscuit untouched, as he told her huskily, 'I don't know about you, but I think it's time we left.'

Charlotte discovered that, although this was the moment she had been waiting for all evening, she suddenly felt extremely nervous, and almost shy.

She nodded, unable to speak, sitting tensely in her chair as Daniel stood up.

CHAPTER SEVEN

THEY had been driving for ten minutes or so before Charlotte realised that Daniel seemed to be taking her straight home.

Confusion battled with disappointment and the sense of acutely sharp rejection. Had she completely misread the situation? Didn't he *want* her after all? Had tonight simply been a way of passing an empty evening?

The car slowed down and she turned to look at him before she realised that they were approaching a crossroads. It was too late to look away again; Daniel was looking back at her.

'I suppose you know how little I want this evening to end,' he told her huskily. 'How much I want... you...'

Charlotte held her breath, too proud to ask him why if he wanted her so much he was taking her home.

'Don't worry. I'm not going to spoil things between us by rushing you into bed before we've had a chance to get to know one another properly... much as I'd like to.'

Him rush *her*. She wondered what he would say if she told him how much she wanted him, but she knew she wasn't going to. She didn't have that kind of courage, that kind of self-confidence.

The road was dark, empty of other traffic, the hedges dark shapes lining the roadside, the car's headlights picking out the hedges and trees and the countryside beyond them.

Neither of them spoke. Charlotte couldn't. She was too aware of the electric tension and disappointment that filled her. Half of her was astounded that she could feel such intense desire, the other half was a little afraid, a little resentful that *she* should be so caught up in such intense emotional and physical needs while Daniel, despite saying that he wanted her, despite implying that he shared her feelings, remained so clearly in control.

And then, completely without warning, she heard him make a sharp sound and the car started to brake. By the time she had turned her head to give him a startled look of interrogation the car had stopped and he was turning to her, saying thickly, 'It's no good...I can't...'

And then she was in his arms and he was holding her, kissing her as she had dreamed of him doing all day.

As he pulled her against him she could feel the fiery heat coming off his body and the tension in his muscles when he touched her face, tracing its contours. His hand trembled slightly and as he kissed her, despite his attempt to be restrained and to hold back, his initial questioning hesitation quickly gave way to a hungry claiming of her mouth that left her in no doubt about his desire for her.

'God, I want you...I want you so much,' he told her between kisses, his hands stroking down over her back, holding her hips, pulling her so close to him that she could feel the rapid-fire thud of his heartbeat.

Her own hands were under his jacket, pressed first flat against his chest and then sliding round to his back as she strained against him.

When his hand cupped her breast she made a soft sound of pleasure against his mouth, her nails tensing against his back, flexing like the pleasured weaving of a cat's paws.

She felt him shudder beneath that tiny reflex response, not knowing whether it was that which caused him to groan her name and mutter how much he needed her, how much he desired her, or the soft feel of her breast within his hand. But when his thumb-tip probed her nipple, stroking its excited hardness, it was her turn to cry out, to twist passionately against him, her movement sharply checked by the realisation that they were still in the car and that the contact she wanted with him was impossible within its confined space.

As he felt her tension Daniel opened his eyes. He was still holding her, but more gently now, rueful realisation in both his face and his voice as he kissed her softly and apologised, 'I'm sorry. I promise you I don't normally behave like this.'

He touched her mouth with his fingertip, tracing its softly swollen shape, his concentration on her compulsive, hungry, his own mouth suddenly softer, fuller, so that she ached to run her tongue-tip along his bottom lip to probe the slight parting of his mouth and to taste the mysterious maleness that lay beyond.

'It's your fault, you know,' he told her. 'Every time I look at you...' He was looking at her now, and she was starting to tremble inwardly and outwardly.

'If only I didn't have quite so much on my plate at the moment,' he groaned, holding her, rocking her gently as he spoke to her. 'That's everyone's complaint these days, isn't it? That there just isn't enough time.'

'Is it the court case?' Charlotte asked him.

He shook his head. 'No.' He paused, looking away from her, his body suddenly tensing slightly. 'No,' he told her sombrely again. 'There's something...a problem which I'm not sure I'm going to be able to resolve. A promise I made an old friend. One I can't ignore and yet at the same time...'

'Do you...? Would it help to talk to me about it?' Charlotte ventured.

Immediately he seemed to withdraw from her, both emotionally and physically, so that she was left feeling as though she had trespassed on to forbidden ground. When she looked at him he was looking straight ahead, his mouth compressed. It was, Charlotte realised helplessly, as though he had suddenly removed himself totally from her, shutting her out. As though, she acknowledged painfully, he did not want to trust her with his confidences.

'I'm sorry, Charlotte,' she heard him apologising. And then he swore under his breath and said angrily, 'Hell, this isn't what I intended at all. There's nothing...nothing I want more right now

than to take you home with me and make love to
you.'

Charlotte was already moving back into her seat,
her hands automatically smoothing her clothes and
her hair while she tried to suppress the feeling of
rejection and misery crawling nauseously through
her.

How had it happened? How had all their loving
intimacy been destroyed so quickly and easily? And
by what? A few words...a sentence or so.

She could feel the hot burn of bitter tears stinging
the backs of her eyes. She blinked them away, de-
riding herself for her vulnerability.

All right, so he had a problem he couldn't discuss
with her. That did not mean that...

That what? That he didn't want her? Oh, no, she
knew that. She knew he wanted her physically at
least, but *she* wanted, needed more from him than
that. She loved him wholly and unreservedly and
she wanted him to love her unreservedly in return,
and she wanted him to trust her as well; to wipe
out the destructive wounds of the last few months,
to heal them with the balm of his professional respect and faith in her.

'I'd better get you home.'

He sounded tired, drained.

'I've got a meeting in chambers tomorrow at
nine.'

'To discuss this secret business you can't discuss
with me?' she asked him, her voice suddenly sharp
and sore.

She could feel him looking at her, but she refused to look back at him.

'No, it's not about that,' he told her. His voice was heavy and dull. She had a brief impulse to turn to him and to reach out to him, to pretend that the last five minutes had simply never happened, to go back to when she was still held in his arms, but he was already setting the car in motion and all the joy and happiness had gone out of the evening for her.

When he stopped the car in her parents' drive he hesitated for a few seconds before moving, and then said huskily, 'I'm sorry if I've spoiled things but...'

As she reached for the door-handle Charlotte told him brittlely, 'It's quite all right. I do understand that some things have to remain confidential between solicitor and client.'

She knew she had to get away before she made a complete fool of herself and told him how much it hurt her that he still obviously didn't trust her. With her head still averted from him she added tersely, 'After all, with my track record, I'm lucky to have a job at all, aren't I, never mind——'

She gasped with shock at the speed with which he reached for her, dragging her against his body, looking at her with such a fierce intensity that her heart started to pound with reckless speed.

'It isn't like that. It isn't like that at all,' he muttered to her as he held her, and then as he looked at her he added rawly, 'I need you so much.'

When he kissed her she knew she should object, make a stand, point out to him that they could not have any kind of worthwhile relationship without mutual trust, but as her senses responded to the command of his mouth they blocked out the mess-

ages from her brain, drawing her down into a
sensual cocoon where nothing existed other than
the way he made her feel.

She had allowed herself to get upset about nothing,
she told herself sleepily later, curled up in bed, re-
living the events of the evening.

She was being over-sensitive again, looking for
problems which did not exist. After all, hadn't
Daniel told her how much he valued her? And tonight he had certainly shown her how much he
wanted her.

He might not have said anything about love, but
she had not expected that. And, after all, neither
had she. Both of them were mature enough to be
wary of using such words too easily, knowing how
quickly they could become devalued and tarnished.

No, what she needed from him now, before he
spoke of love to her, was to hear him tell her that
he had been wrong about her; to hear him tell her
that she need feel no guilt for her failures and that
in no way did it reflect on her abilities.

Her mouth twisted a little. No doubt his great-
aunt Lydia would have despised her for such a
weakness.

In the morning Charlotte told herself firmly that
she had to put the past behind her, and she drove
to work clinging firmly to the memory of Daniel
telling her how much he valued her, rather than
allowing herself to dwell on the doubts she had suffered the previous evening.

Since she knew that Daniel had a meeting in chambers first thing, she was not surprised by his absence.

Anne, hurrying into her office with the post, told her briefly, 'Oh, by the way, Daniel won't be in until later.'

'Yes, I know,' she responded automatically, picking up the post, only aware of the way Anne was looking at her when she sensed her surprise from her stillness.

Anne said nothing, but Charlotte had seen the brief look of speculation in her eyes, and without knowing why she should feel it necessary she told her hurriedly, 'He... Daniel rang me at home last night to tell me he had a meeting in chambers this morning.'

'Ah. I wondered how you knew, because the clerk to the barrister only rang *me* late yesterday to warn me that the meeting had had to be brought forward because Mr Oliver was due in court.'

There was no real reason why Anne should not know that she had had dinner with Daniel last night, Charlotte reminded herself later, but the discovery of her feelings for him, the complete change-round in their relationship, was still so new that she wanted to hug it to herself, to keep it as her own special secret, to be explored and enjoyed in complete privacy.

Because she perhaps still didn't believe it was happening herself... Because maybe she still did not entirely believe...

Believe what? That Daniel *wanted* her? she demanded quickly of herself, firmly refusing to dwell on her other doubts, firmly suppressing them, reminding herself that only this morning she had promised herself that she would think positively; that she would look forward to the future instead of dwelling on the past.

Charlotte worked hard all morning, congratulating herself on recalling a very obscure precedent that was relevant to one of their cases.

She had just come downstairs from the practice's small reference library where she had been checking up on it when Anne came into her office, her normally placid face creased into an angry scowl.

'Something wrong?' Charlotte asked her.

'It's that woman.'

'What woman?'

'That Winters woman,' Anne told her explosively. 'I went to get myself a cup of tea and when I got back I found her prowling round Daniel's office. Ginny had tried to tell her that he wasn't in. Honestly, I don't know why Daniel puts up with her.'

'Well, she is a client,' Charlotte pointed out mildly, but inside she could feel her stomach muscles clenching a little.

'You mean she *was*. Probate on her late husband's estate was granted weeks ago, but she still keeps coming in here, demanding to see Daniel. And she never even attempts to make a proper appointment. Of course, we all know what she's after, but what mystifies me is why Daniel lets her get away with it.

'I mean, I know she's rich, and I suppose she's sexy as well, if you like human predators, but I thought Daniel had more taste. I know we've all joked about the way she's been chasing him, but up until recently I never thought there was actually anything serious in it.'

'And now you do?' Charlotte asked her calmly, while her heart thumped inside her chest with leaden dread.

Anne shrugged.

'Well, what else are we supposed to think? As I say, Paul Winters's will was simple enough. She got everything. That was a bit of a shock, though. Paul had a stepson from his first marriage, and he and Gordon were very close until she came along. He took over running the business when Paul retired and I think everyone expected that he would leave control of it to Gordon, instead of which he never even got a mention in the will.

'There was some gossip that he and Paul had a quarrel when Paul married Patricia. Men. They just don't seem capable of seeing what's under their noses, do they? Especially when it comes as sexily packaged as Patricia.

'Anyway, I managed to get rid of her. I told her that it was unlikely that Daniel would be back today.

'Is anything wrong?' she asked Charlotte.

'What? No, no,' Charlotte lied brittlely. 'I was just wondering why Daniel took on this case.'

'Oh, which one is that?'

'The Calvin case,' Charlotte told her, fighting to keep her voice steady.

Anne's comments had shocked and upset her. Surely Daniel would not be behaving with her in the way that he was if he was already romantically involved with someone else? And yet *why*, if Anne was right and the estate had been wound up, did he continue to allow Patricia Winters to monopolise so much of his time?

'The Calvin case?' Anne looked at the file on her desk. 'Oh, yes, that's the one where our client is suing his employers for not allowing him parity with their female employees when it comes to maternity leave.'

'Yes,' Charlotte agreed, her smile and her voice tight as she added, 'It will be an interesting test case. But I can't see us winning it.'

'No,' Anne agreed. 'But then, it's typical of Daniel to take on a case like that.'

'More media coverage and publicity,' Charlotte suggested drily.

Anne gave her an uncertain look, and then shook her head. 'Daniel isn't like that,' she told her positively. 'He's more interested in winning justice than in making money. You wouldn't believe the number of cases he takes on which are outside the legal aid requirements and which he knows he'll never be properly paid for. But he always says that establishing someone's right to justice is more important than a large fee. Of course, it helps that we do get a lot of healthily profitable business.'

'Yes,' Charlotte agreed. 'Philanthropy does have to be financed.'

Why was it that she was being subjected to this constant see-sawing of emotion, one moment seeing Daniel as devious, his true motives hidden, the next being forced to recognise his generosity and his concern for his fellow man . . . and woman . . . ? Especially one woman, she reflected darkly, at least if Anne's chatty confidences had been anything to go by.

When Anne had gone she pushed aside her work and got up to stare out of the window.

Think this through logically, she told herself. All right, so maybe Daniel was flattered by Patricia Winters's interest, maybe he might even have encouraged it—after all, he knew *her* before you came on the scene. It doesn't mean that because he might have had a relationship with her he is *still* involved with her.

But he had been taking her out to dinner the night she and Sarah had gone out together, she reminded herself, and he had described her then as a client, when, if Anne was to be believed, their solicitor-client relationship was over.

He could quite easily be acting for her in some other capacity, she reminded herself. If she was so concerned, all she needed to do was to ask him.

And yet she knew that she couldn't. Her confidence was not such that she had the courage to question him about his previous relationships. They hadn't known one another long enough—their relationship wasn't sufficiently well established.

What relationship? she asked herself fiercely. Maybe he *was* just amusing himself with her; maybe . . .

Stop being stupid, she warned herself. He simply isn't that kind of man.

She comforted herself with that knowledge as she sat down, but then an inner voice asked her cynically if she was sure she knew him well enough to make that kind of statement.

Why did she have to torment herself with these doubts? she asked herself angrily as she went back to her work. Why couldn't she simply accept things at face value? Why did she feel this nagging sense of uncertainty and unease?

Halfway through the afternoon Daniel returned. Charlotte could hear him dictating to Anne when she came downstairs from the 'nursery'.

She heard him thank Anne, and then the door opening as the other girl left. She wanted to get up and go through to his office, to assure herself that she had not dreamed what had happened between them last night, but suddenly she felt too self-conscious, too shy almost to do so.

'Busy?'

The warm sound of his voice made her tense as he walked into her office. He came and stood beside her, not leaning over her as he usually did. She looked up at him, her throat suddenly tense, her mouth dry.

This was it. He was going to tell her that last night had been a mistake, that——

'Did I tell you last night how much I enjoyed being with you?' he asked her softly.

She couldn't help it; she knew her relief, her happiness must be visible to him on her face. 'Did...did the court case go well?' she asked him huskily, unable to make any other response.

'We won.' He paused for a moment and then added wryly, 'I suppose you're right. The office isn't the place to discuss personal matters.'

When she looked up he was smiling at her, and she had a mad impulse to tell him how she felt about him, to tell him how confused and hurt she felt, but instead she heard herself saying shakily, 'I've been doing some research on the Fielding case, and I think I've found the precedent that may help us.'

'You have? Great. Come on through to my office and bring the file with you. We'll have a look at it.'

His desk was much larger than hers and while she watched he pulled a chair up next to his own, waving her into it.

As she sat down she saw that there was a file on the desk in front of her. At first she thought it was the papers for the case he had just been in court on, and then she recognised Patricia Winters's name on it.

'Mrs Winters was in earlier looking for you,' she commented, hoping that her voice wouldn't betray her feelings.

'Yes, Anne told me.'

Daniel's voice had suddenly become terse and sharp, but she ignored the warning it held, impelled to plunge on. 'She seems to come here a lot. Is there some problem with her late husband's estate?'

She held her breath as she waited for him to reply, her heart thumping heavily as she acknowledged her own duplicity with a sick feeling of self-contempt. *Why* was she trying to trap him like this? Why didn't she simply ask him outright what she wanted to know?

For a moment she thought he wasn't going to reply, he was silent for so long, or was it simply in her imagination that the silence seemed to stretch like taut wire? Was he actually watching her as sharply as she felt, as though he could see inside her head, as though he *knew* what she was trying to do? Could he even perhaps *know* that she was perfectly well aware that the estate had been wound up already?

She was beginning to tell herself that she was a fool and that any minute now he was going to challenge her with her duplicity, when he said brusquely, 'You could say that.' And then, as she stared in shocked disbelief from his face to the file, he reached across her and picked it up, opening one of the drawers in his desk, putting the file in it and then locking it, his actions as brutal as though he had physically struck her.

Charlotte couldn't believe it. It had all happened so quickly, the lie falling so patly from his lips. And he had lied to her. Why on earth hadn't he said something else? If he had to deceive her, why couldn't he have chosen something more plausible—why couldn't he have told her that he was acting on some other matter for Patricia Winters? Why choose the one lie that could so easily be proved not to be true?

As she sat there, numb with pain and disbelief, she was conscious of him speaking to her, but she was too distraught to take in anything that he was saying.

He had lied to her, coldly and deliberately. And why? Why? Because there was no client relationship with Patricia Winters and because he didn't want her to know the truth.

Somehow or other she must have managed to appear calm and normal, her responses the right ones, despite the turmoil she was suffering inside.

It was only when she got up to go back to her own office and he reached out to stop her, his hand on her arm, that her control almost broke as she fought not to jerk away from him, not to tell him not to touch her.

'I've got a dinner engagement this evening,' he told her. 'But I thought this weekend——'

'No.' Her denial was sharp and immediate, causing him to frown and look narrowly at her.

'Charlotte, is something wrong? Last night... if I offended you, took things too fast...'

She could feel herself starting to tremble. He sounded so sincere, so full of concern for her. If she had to stay here much longer she would be screaming her anguish at him, telling him how much he was hurting her, telling him that her feelings for him were such that she wanted him exclusively, that she did not, could not be someone with whom he indulged in a covert and undoubtedly brief affair.

Hot tears of longing and shame were already stinging her eyes. She had to get away from him before she lost control completely. She felt sick with despair and misery, but somehow she managed to retain just enough control to deny sharply, 'No. No, it's nothing like that.'

She had turned and was walking quickly away from him when he caught up with her.

'Charlotte, this weekend——'

'I can't. I... I've made other plans,' she lied hoarsely.

She couldn't bear to look at him in case he saw the misery in her eyes.

His hand dropped away from her arm, his own voice cool and remote now as he said quietly, 'Yes. I see. Well, perhaps another time, then.'

Only pausing to drop her file on her desk, Charlotte bolted for the sanctuary of the ladies', relieved to find that the room was empty.

She stayed there until the trembling had stopped, and the sickness churning through her stomach had subsided.

And then, as she checked her reflection in the mirror, she couldn't help contrasting it with the way she had looked this morning.

It wasn't *all* Daniel's fault, she told herself wearily. By her own impulsive actions she had allowed him to think that she was willing . . . that she wanted . . .

But that had been when she had believed. When she had believed what? That she was the only woman in his life . . . that there could be something special between them.

What a complete fool she had been.

CHAPTER EIGHT

IT WAS no good, she could not take the coward's way out and hand in her notice, Charlotte told herself drearily after a weekend spent compulsively going over and over what had happened. She had received a bank statement on Saturday morning and it had stunned her to discover that the high level of interest rates had meant that for all her efforts she had barely managed to reduce her personal borrowing at all.

There was no way she could morally or financially give up her job. She would just have to grit her teeth and get on with it.

On Monday morning when she went to work she was wan-faced and hollow-eyed.

So much fresh stress on top of that which she had already previously suffered was making her feel jumpy and on edge, her nerves and her emotions raw with pain.

But for once it seemed luck was with her. Daniel had had to go to London, where he was acting in conjunction with another solicitor.

'One of the new clients we picked up following the publicity on the Vitalle case,' Richard told her when he came into her office. 'Are you all right?' he asked her. 'Not working you too hard, are we?'

Charlotte shook her head.

She had lunch with Margaret, who was complaining about the problems she was having with the 'nursery'.

'Honestly, sometimes you'd think they *were* still children and not young adults.'

'Perhaps being relegated to the "nursery" doesn't exactly help—give a dog a bad name and all that,' Charlotte suggested.

'Mm, you could be right. Or maybe I'm just getting old. When's Daniel back, by the way?'

'I don't know,' Charlotte told her brusquely, and then wished she hadn't been quite so sharp as she saw the way Margaret frowned.

She couldn't sleep, she could barely eat and as though that weren't enough her body was behaving as though *she* was its enemy and not Daniel.

She woke up in the night with the taste of his kisses still on her lips, aching with wanting him while she tried helplessly to remind herself of all the reasons she had for not doing so.

It wasn't so bad during the day. At least then she could exercise some kind of control over her thoughts and her body by grimly reminding herself of Patricia Winters, but at night she had no such defences. In her sleep her senses overruled reality and tortured her instead with dreams that were a collection of memories and wishes interlocked with love and desire.

Was it really any wonder that others were beginning to comment on how strained and tired she looked? The trouble was that, no matter how much she told herself that she should do so, she could not stop loving Daniel.

And then midway through the week, a day earlier than anyone had expected, he came back.

He looked as tense as she felt, Charlotte acknowledged with shock when she saw him. There was no sign of his normal smile, and his eyes were cold and empty. He looked and behaved like a man on automatic pilot.

'Is your car here?' he asked Charlotte as he walked into her office.

When she nodded, he said curtly, 'Good, I need it and you.'

And then, before she could say another word, he was walking out of her office, obviously expecting her to follow him.

Her car was parked in the square. She paused outside it, looking uncertainly at Daniel.

'No, you drive,' he told her, adding quietly, 'It's John Balfour. He died late last night. The home rang me in London this morning. He'd been ill for a few days—that was why I'd given them my number. They need me to go through his things . . . I'm his executor.'

He sounded tired and defeated, and as she unlocked the car Charlotte saw illuminatingly that it wasn't just a client he had lost, but someone whom he had looked upon as a friend.

Silently she got into the car.

'I caught the first train back I could. I suppose I could have gone home for my car, but to be honest right now I don't think I'd be the world's safest driver.'

'John meant a lot to you,' Charlotte ventured.

'Yes. If you like, he was my last link with Lydia. They were close friends. Maybe at one time they were even lovers—I don't know.'

Fortunately Charlotte could remember the way to the home. She was acutely conscious of Daniel sitting silently beside her, his thoughts obviously with John Balfour.

Compassion for him overwhelmed her, drowning out her anger against him. Maybe he did not love her; maybe he *had* been guilty of deceiving her, but there could be no doubts about his feelings for the man who had just died.

Once they reached the home they were shown quickly and silently up to John Balfour's room.

Without its occupant, it seemed sad and somehow incomplete. If *she* felt his absence so strongly after one meeting with him, then how must Daniel feel? Charlotte asked herself as she watched in silence while Daniel moved slowly about the room.

'He didn't have very many possessions,' the matron was telling Daniel. 'Just what you can see, and the contents of his desk, and of course the furniture—we let them bring a few of their own pieces when they come here. It helps them to settle in. And then, of course, there's his deed box.'

The matron left, and, as she watched Daniel going carefully, painfully almost, through the drawers in the large old-fashioned bureau, Charlotte wondered why he had needed to bring her with him.

'Does he ... did he have much family?' she asked uncertainly, unable to bear a silence which held such a deep quality of sadness and pain.

'Distant cousins, that's all. His things can be put in storage for the time being. I've got space enough for them at home.' He had removed a key from one of the desk drawers and now he looked round, frowning, and then went over to the bed, reaching under it to withdraw a heavy wooden chest.

Someone had brought a tray of tea while he'd been going through the desk, and now Charlotte poured it. Her hostility towards him, the pain he had caused her, was temporarily held in check, overwhelmed by her awareness of his emotional reaction to John Balfour's death.

No one could fail to be moved by his obvious sadness. It was evident in the way he had touched the few ornaments and the silver photograph frames, in the way he had carefully and slowly, reverently almost, gone through the contents of the desk.

Had these been her treasures, her few belongings, she could not have wished for them to have been treated with greater care and emotion, Charlotte recognised as she swallowed hard on the lump in her throat.

Daniel, she noticed, had suddenly gone very still. He was holding a pile of letters, his expression very bleak.

'What is it...what's wrong?' Charlotte asked him.

He shook his head. 'These letters were written by Lydia. I recognise her handwriting. It's odd, isn't it, how differently we feel when it's someone we know and love who's involved in something like this rather than someone from whom we are detached?

'Logic and training tells me that these letters should at least be preserved, if not read, and yet instinct, emotion says that they are private...meant for one person's eyes alone, and that no one but that person should ever see them.

'My father wanted me to train as a barrister, you know,' he told her abruptly. 'But Lydia advised me not to. She and my father quarrelled over it. He thought it was because she wanted me, a third generation, to go into the practice she had started, but it wasn't that. She didn't believe that I had the right temperament, the necessary degree of detachment required to become a good barrister. In those days she knew me better than I knew myself.'

He looked at the letters again, and, sensing what he intended to do, Charlotte reached out towards him, impelled by instinct rather than logic.

'Keep them,' she told him huskily. '*You* might feel that you were too close to your great-aunt to want to read them, but future generations who did not know her personally, your children, your grandchildren...think of what you might be depriving them by destroying them.'

He paused and looked at her.

'My children?' He sounded oddly bitter, angry almost. 'Somehow I don't think...' He stopped and looked at the letters again, and then, to her shock, he suddenly held them out to her and told her tautly, 'Very well, then, you make the decision.'

She caught the letters awkwardly as he tossed them towards her. 'But I can't... I don't...' she stammered huskily. 'She isn't...'

'You're a woman,' he told her. 'And a solicitor. What would you have wanted in Lydia's shoes?'

He had turned away from her, and was going through some other papers.

He couldn't have meant it, Charlotte decided. He could not possibly have meant to entrust *her* of all people with that kind of decision.

She knew how much his great-aunt had meant to him. How much he had loved her. To ask *her*, whom he did not trust professionally and whom he certainly could not respect as a woman, to be the one to make such a decision... She looked at him. He still had his back towards her.

She ought to protest—Lydia had been *his* great-aunt—but then while she looked at him she saw the way his hand trembled as he held the papers and she was filled with a soft flood of loving compassion.

She tucked the bundle of letters into her shoulder-bag and then drank her tea, quietly allowing Daniel time to come to terms with his emotions.

It was over half an hour before he spoke again.

'I think we've done everything we can here,' he pronounced. 'The home will arrange the practical details of the funeral.'

He hadn't touched his tea, but Charlotte did not try to point this out to him, just as she refrained from asking him why he had needed her help when she had done nothing other than simply be there with him.

They walked in silence towards her car, and then when they reached it and she was unlocking it Daniel turned to her and said rawly, 'Thank you.'

For what? she wanted to ask him, but the words stuck in her throat. This was a different side of him, a vulnerable unexpected side she had never expected to see him reveal, least of all to her.

'I'm afraid I'm going to have to ask you to give me a lift home,' he told her when she had unlocked the car.

'That's no problem,' Charlotte assured him, 'but I shall have to ask you for directions. I've no idea where you live.'

She looked at him as she finished speaking and was surprised at the expression on his face.

It was a mixture of bitterness and pain, although she had no idea why her logical comment should have provoked such a look. Unless perhaps he was still thinking about John and Lydia, but his next words seemed to contradict that thought.

'No, you don't, do you?' he told her flatly, and as she turned the key in the ignition and started her car she wondered why on earth her lack of awareness of where he lived should affect him so emotionally.

The clear and concise directions he gave her were easy to follow. He lived on the opposite side of town from her parents, and not, she was rather surprised to discover, in a part of the area which was locally known to be *the* place to live, but instead much further out than she had expected, in fact beyond the ring of small villages which surrounded the town and out in the open countryside.

'I'm afraid it's rather a long way to drag you,' he commented when they had driven through a tiny hamlet and he had told her that it wasn't much further. 'I hope I'm not interfering with any plans you might have made for the evening.'

Charlotte shook her head.

'It's left here,' Daniel told her, indicating a small lane that led off the main road.

The lane had a bumpy uneven surface, and looked as though it was only used by local farmers.

Charlotte had no idea what kind of home she had expected Daniel to have; perhaps one of the smart newly renovated town houses in the town itself, or perhaps a comfortable Victorian or Edwardian detached house with its own grounds; the kind normally described as a 'comfortable family home'.

Certainly what she had not expected was the renovated and extended barn she could now see at the bottom of the lane.

'An impulse buy,' Daniel told her as though he had read her mind. 'I saw it three summers ago and fell in love with it. The people who had bought it and drawn up the plans for the original renovations were moving abroad. You can't see it from this side, but the far side of the house is mostly glass; it faces south and has the most incredible views. Something about the place drew me, attracted me— perhaps it was the quality of the light. In the summer it's almost magical, that combination of sunlight and old wood.'

At the front the barn was built of soft, warm-coloured brick, its windows small and lead-paned.

There was a cobbled drive to one side down which she drove, and over the top of the low clipped hedge she could see a pretty country-style front garden with a path running down to a small gate, green lawns and blowzy tousled flowerbeds which in summer she imagined would be filled with a heady scented mixture of old-fashioned perennials.

She had stopped the car, and was waiting for Daniel to get out, but suddenly he turned to her and said huskily, 'Have supper with me, Charlotte.'

Have supper with *him*?

She stared at him, confused by his invitation, her heart starting to race, her senses responding helplessly to him as he turned towards her in the confines of her small car.

She could smell the heat of his body, its maleness, its tiredness; she could see the pain the events of the day had etched alongside his eyes and his mouth.

She knew without his having to say it why he didn't want to be alone.

She wanted to protest that she wasn't an anodyne, a deterrent to be used to hold at bay emotions he didn't want to endure, but as fast as she tried to reach out for common sense and logic they slipped away from her.

Her fingers, apparently possessing the will to make their own decisions, reached to unclip her seatbelt and to turn off the engine, to open the car door, her leg muscles developing the same free will apparently, because, without intending to do so, she discovered that she was standing outside her car and locking it.

'It's this way.'

Daniel was standing next to her, ushering her along the cobbled drive and to the rear of the house.

Daylight was beginning to fade, but there was enough of it left for her to catch her breath in delight as she saw what he had meant about the house's windows.

In between the heavy ancient oak timbers and the soft mellowness of the country brick the architect had designed what was virtually a wall of glass, broken up only by the original timbers and brick, their softness muting the glass's starkness so that the combination of ancient and modern designs blended softly one into the other.

Daniel had unlocked the door.

'Come in,' he invited, switching on the lights as Charlotte followed him into a roomy kitchen.

Here again beams and brickwork had been left exposed. A bright red Aga filled what must have originally been a huge fireplace; the kitchen units were built of oak, their surface left unstained and limed.

The stone-flagged floor, polished and uneven by the passage of time, should have been cold but wasn't. It was easy to imagine a family inhabiting this room, living, laughing, loving this place of rich contrasting textures and materials.

It *wasn't* easy, though, to imagine Patricia Winters in such a setting, Charlotte reflected as she glanced around her homely surroundings.

'Well, what's your verdict?'

Daniel's soft question startled her. She froze, her face flushing as she wondered how on earth he had known what she was thinking, and then she realised that he was referring to the house itself and not to Patricia Winters's place in it.

'It...it's...it's wonderful,' she told him.

His face creased into a warm smile.

'Just wait until you see the view from upstairs,' he told her. 'It's awe-inspiring. Especially first thing in the morning, just as the sun's starting to rise...'

They were looking at one another and neither of them, it seemed, was able to look away.

Her mouth, Charlotte discovered, had gone very dry. She could feel the fast fierce beat of her heart pulsing into her throat. A shivery mixture of tension and excitement invaded her body, locking her muscles, churning her stomach.

Was it her imagination, or could she actually smell the scent of Daniel's skin? A fierce shudder went through her, visibly shaking her body.

'Now that you've agreed to have supper with me I'd better check that there *is* actually something for us to eat.'

The words were mundane enough, commonplace really, but the huskiness in Daniel's voice had much the same physical effect on her as though he had actually touched her over-sensitive skin.

She saw him move...watched as he opened the fridge door, heard him saying something about pasta, heard her own muted shaky response, watched as he started to remove food from the fridge and the cupboards, all without moving herself...without being able to move.

What was *wrong* with her? She had been alone enough times with him before without experiencing this kind of reaction. All right, so she desired him, loved him, but this total overwhelming of her senses, this swamping of her mental logical processes to the point where every particle of her that was capable of doing *anything* was concentrating exclusively on watching him, on absorbing everything that she could about him, this was not something that she was familiar with, and it was certainly not something she knew how to counter.

She was helpless beneath its onslaught, totally caught up in the intensity of it, becalmed in its motionless endless sea.

She could smell the ripe warm scent of tomatoes, the fresh sharp tang of herbs, the rich aroma of meat, each scent as new to her, as sharp as though she had never experienced them before.

Daniel poured them both a glass of wine; as he handed hers to her Charlotte focused helplessly on him. Beneath its taut maleness his skin was slightly flushed ... The heat of the Aga perhaps. She could feel the warmth of the glass where his fingers had touched it. She lifted the wine to her lips and drank unsteadily.

The wine was rough and warm, and even without closing her eyes she could imagine the Italian countryside; the warm terracottas of its earth and its buildings, the dark cool green of its cypress.

What was wrong with her? Why was she experiencing these things so clearly, so sharply?

She watched as Daniel moved back to the Aga.

He hadn't asked for her help. He cooked economically and easily, as though it was a task with which he was long familiar. His movements were

mercifully free of the showiness she had so often
seen in those of Bevan's friends who had boasted
of their culinary talents. Daniel was no 'new man'
showing off his skills to an impressed and admiring
female audience.

He turned to look at her, as though aware of her
scrutiny, his concentration on her momentarily
breaking her free of her isolation.

'Can I help?' she asked him uncertainly. 'The
table...?'

He shook his head.

'We'll eat in the sitting-room. There's a fire in
there. I'll go and switch it on if you'll just keep an
eye on this for me for a moment.'

As she walked over to him she was aware of her
heightened sensitivity towards him. It was as though
her senses were a finely tuned computer, capable
of the most complex monitoring.

While he was gone she tried to shake herself free
of her own vulnerability.

He wanted her company *now*, she reminded
herself, but she would be a fool to imagine that she
had any real place in his life.

The moment he came back into the room she was
aware of it.

'It's almost ready,' he told her.

She could smell the food and knew that she ought
to be hungry, but she was too aware of him, her
senses too filled by that awareness to leave room
for anything else.

When their meal was ready Daniel loaded everything on to a sturdy oak trolley.

'The sitting-room is this way,' he told Charlotte.

She followed him out of the kitchen and into a rectangular inner hall which seemed to bisect the house. Its beamed walls had soft cream plaster infills; an old, well-polished oak chest stood against one wall. There was a portrait of a woman hanging on the wall above it, her features illuminated by a light.

'Lydia,' Daniel informed Charlotte as she paused to look at it.

She could see the family resemblance, softened in Lydia Jefferson's feminine features. The portrait had obviously been painted when she was a young woman. Her hair was the same rich dark brown as Daniel's, the shape of the nose, the firmness of her jaw his as well.

'You're very alike,' she told him.

'In looks a little, but I'm afraid I don't have Lydia's foresight, nor her determination. I doubt that in her shoes I could ever have achieved what she achieved. I don't think I could make that kind of sacrifice.'

'Sacrifice?' Charlotte questioned him, puzzled.

'Yes. She gave up everything to prove a point, to prove that she could be as successful a solicitor as her male contemporaries. She refused to marry because she was afraid that if she did her husband might try to persuade her to abandon her practice. She believed that it was impossible to be both a practising solicitor and a wife and mother. In her day, after all, no one had heard that it was possible to "have it all".'

He sounded so grim that Charlotte turned away from the portrait to look at him.

'And do you agree with her that women cannot have it all?' she challenged him.

He looked at her.

'I don't think that *anyone*, man or woman, can. I think whatever one chooses in life there are sacrifices to be made. John Balfour loved Lydia, and I suspect that she loved him. In John's room this afternoon, I couldn't help thinking, wondering. It seems such a waste, to have loved one another and yet to have deliberately turned their backs on that love for whatever reason.'

Charlotte stared at him. These were not the kind of words, the kind of emotions she had expected from him. She could certainly not envisage Bevan ever making that kind of statement.

He had opened a door and was indicating that she was to precede him through it.

The room that lay beyond it was large and comfortably furnished. All along one wall were the huge sheets of glass where once presumably there must have been lath and plaster infill panels and perhaps bricks. The wooden floor glowed warmly in the light from the fire and from the lamps dotted around the room.

In one corner Charlotte could see a baby grand piano.

Daniel saw her looking at it. 'It was Lydia's,' he explained. 'When she was growing up children were taught to play the piano as a matter of course. She wanted me to learn but I'm afraid I never got beyond the finger-exercise stage.'

Two comfortable-looking settees covered in a striped fabric in toning creams and rusts faced one another across the fire. Terracotta rugs softened the polished expanse of the wooden floor.

As Daniel pushed the trolley in front of the fire Charlotte saw that it had good-sized extensions which made it large enough to use as a table.

'Let's eat this while it's still hot,' he suggested.

Charlotte sat down. She still wasn't really hungry, but she picked up her plate automatically, shaking her head when Daniel asked her if she would like him to refill her wine glass.

'Better not, with me driving,' she told him.

He gave her a wry smile. 'No, I'm sorry, I was forgetting.'

He had been about to refill his own glass, but now he put the bottle down, and once again Charlotte was struck by not just his consideration for other people, but also his awareness. It wasn't a trait she could ever remember encountering in a man, and it was certainly not one that Bevan had ever displayed. All men, she had long ago decided, possessed a certain instinctive animal selfishness, seldom displayed to women, who almost from birth were more aware of the needs of others.

Charlotte ate as much as she could, but she was less than halfway through her meal when she had to admit that she couldn't eat any more.

To her surprise, when she looked at him, she realised that Daniel too seemed to be struggling with his food.

'Not hungry?' he asked her.

She shook her head. 'No, I'm sorry, I don't seem to be.'

She started to stand up, an odd panicky sensation building up inside her, an awareness of the intimacy of their surroundings and her own vulnerability coupled with a sudden sharp need to get completely away.

Perhaps because of this, or perhaps because she moved too quickly, her head spun dizzily as she moved.

Daniel pushed the trolley aside and came towards her.

'Charlotte...'

She hadn't realised he was quite so close to her, her eyes registering her startled awareness of his proximity and with it her apprehension.

'Charlotte.' He said her name again, his voice husky and raw.

Charlotte looked at him, unable to stop herself from responding to what she could hear in his voice.

He looked back at her, his eyes dark, glittering slightly as they met hers.

Her mouth went dry, the way it had done when she first walked into the kitchen. Her heart was pounding far too fast. She wanted to breathe deeply to steady herself, but she couldn't seem to do so.

She looked helplessly at Daniel and knew that he was going to kiss her.

There were a dozen things she could have done, a dozen ways she could have easily and simply avoided what was going to happen, but instead she simply stood there, watching, waiting... *wanting*, so that her very stillness was a kind of subtle encouragement and invitation as well as an acceptance.

He kissed her slowly, hesitantly almost, and she could feel the fine thrill of sensation that went through her. His hands touched her face, cupping it, holding her as his mouth moved more urgently on her own. She could feel the tension in his body, hear the sharp, fierce sound of his breathing, and she knew long before he said it that he wanted her.

He *wanted* her; that was all, she told herself, but she was long past listening to such voices of caution.

Her body had responded to him the moment he had touched her, and had, if she was honest with herself, been aware of him, wanting him, aching for him, long, long before that second.

He touched her gently, carefully, as though she was something rare and precious, and her senses responded helplessly to that message even while her brain fought to deny it.

She just wasn't strong enough, her tortured senses derided her; where she could have resisted him, it was her own needs, her own emotions she could not deny.

She wanted him, loved him too much.

If he had touched her roughly, greedily, selfishly it might have been different, but he wasn't doing any of those things, and her body shivered, helpless with delight and awe as he stroked her throat, his mouth warm and careful as he explored her soft skin, and then suddenly less careful, more hungry, wanting her, needing her as he drew her closely against him so that she could feel not just the fine tremor of desire that pulsed through his body but also its open arousal.

He kissed her again, blindly seeking her mouth, tasting it, possessing it, so that her senses quickened and she was caught, trapped in the drowning tide of her desire.

Behind her tightly closed eyelids, images shivered tormentingly, his skin against hers, his hands touching her, stroking her as he implored her to touch him in turn, both of them lost fathoms deep in their need for one another.

They were images she no longer had the power to resist. She moved closer to him, small keening noises escaping from her throat, silenced by the hot urgent pressure of his mouth, but registered by him nevertheless, his hand on her throat, his thumb monitoring the vibrations of her vocal need.

Charlotte had never felt like this before, never experienced this overwhelming sense of needing to be so much a part of another human being that need simply overwhelmed and outstripped everything else.

She wanted to be close to him, part of him, free of the restrictions of her clothes, able to touch him, to caress him, to feel his hands on her skin.

Her body, normally something to which she paid little attention in the sensual way, was suddenly something of which she was sharply conscious and femalely proud, her awareness of the softness of her skin, the sleekness of her muscles, the curves and the plains of her body all equally sharp as her knowledge of the way her breasts had swollen, her nipples sensitive and erect, the way her stomach muscles had tensed, her body soft and moist, her perceptions sharply focused on the inner physical world of her senses.

And she was equally intensely aware of Daniel, of the hard male thud of his heartbeat, of the heat coming off his body, of the scent of that heat, male and musky, and of the way she was reacting to it, her senses excited by it. She wanted to hold him, to stroke him, to touch his flesh with her hands, to taste the salty damp heat of his skin, to explore it with the delicate sensitivity of her tongue-tip, absorbing each nuance of texture, scent and taste.

She had never known this intensity of desire before, this complexity of emotions and hungers.

Sex, the sex of her late teens and early twenties, had been an uncomplicated straightforward experience, lacking in any of the compelling subtleties she was experiencing now.

Without knowing how she had such knowledge, she felt her body thrill at the thought of licking her way along his throat and over his chest, of feeling the crazed frantic race of his heartbeat, of hearing already in her senses his raw cry of arousal and need as she teased her tongue against his small hard nipple.

She was trembling with all that her senses were relaying to her, her skin bathed in an unfamiliar damp heat.

Somehow, without being aware of doing so, she had slid her hands inside his jacket, and now she became aware that he was trying to shrug himself out of it, while still kissing her.

She helped him as best she could, bemused by the fierce encouraging sounds he was making against her mouth, sounds without any logical meaning and yet which her senses had no trouble in interpreting and responding to.

His skin beneath his shirt was hot, burning almost. He lifted one hand from her hip, where he had been holding her tightly against his body, and started to unfasten the buttons on his shirt.

'Help me, Charlotte,' he begged her huskily. 'God, I want to hold you so much, to feel your skin.'

He stopped speaking as he felt the fierce response of her kiss, a kiss she had not known herself capable of giving, a challenging, demanding kiss that spoke of her needs and hungers as a woman.

His shirt was half undone, and when she opened her eyes, her eyelids heavy and weighted with desire, she could see the criss-crossing of dark hair against his skin.

She touched him exploratively, her fingertips absorbing the damp heat of his flesh.

When she looked at him his face was flushed, his pupils dilated. The way he was looking at her made her heart jump crazily and her body tremble.

Without knowing she had even made the decision to do so, she discovered that she was unfastening the rest of the buttons on his shirt, slowly and hungrily, giving him fierce biting kisses that slowly gentled and grew longer when her hands were finally free to touch him.

It wasn't until she explored the hard bones of his shoulders, pushing his shirt free of them, that she realised it was still buttoned at his cuffs.

As she reached down to unfasten them she kissed the inside of his arm, so totally absorbed by the newness of the sensation she was experiencing that she was barely aware of the frustration he was feeling until she heard the wrench of cloth and realised that in the struggle to free himself completely of his shirt he had torn it.

'Now,' he told her throatily as he took hold of her, 'now you can torment and tease me as much as you like, but I promise you that if you do *I'm* going to retaliate.'

Torment him... tease him... Charlotte gave him a baffled look. Didn't he realise that it was simply her need to touch him that was motivating her? Did he really think she was trying to...?

She went still as she felt his hands on her body, removing her blouse, unzipping her skirt, touching her skin, stroking it. And then abruptly she started to tremble, almost falling against him as pleasure surged through her.

She shivered as he picked her up, but lay quiescent against him as he carried her over to one of the settees, watching him gravely as he lowered her on to it and then slowly removed the rest of her clothes.

There was enough light in the room for him to see her quite clearly, but she felt no disquiet or embarrassment.

She wanted him to look at her, she recognised. She wanted to see the desire darkening his eyes, the heat burning up under his skin. She wanted to see the way his muscles quivered as he fought to control his reaction to her. She wanted to see the way his throat tensed as he swallowed, she wanted to hear the husky male words of praise and pleasure he lavished on her as he kissed her mouth and his hands stroked softly over her skin, their texture slightly rough, totally erotic.

When he cupped her breasts she reached out to cover his hands with her own, her back arching, her body shuddering with pleasure.

He kissed her mouth and then her throat, removing his hands from her body so that she cried out in protest, opening her eyes to see that he was removing the remainder of his own clothes.

She watched him, absorbed in the male perfection of him. His body was taut and firmly muscled, his skin sleek with the gleam of good health, inviting her touch with its sensual message of warmth and pleasure. The dark roughness of his body hair excited and faintly shocked her, her view of it different somehow in this context from what she would have expected had she merely seen him on some beach, her senses so much more sensually aware so that already she knew how when he moved against her in the intimate rhythm of possession the slight abrasion of that roughness would arouse her sensitive flesh.

He turned towards her, watching her, hesitant almost so that she automatically reached out to him, opening her arms to him, her eyes hugely brilliant with all that she was feeling as he took hold of her, whispering her name, kissing her, his body pressed so intimately against her own that she could feel the soft relaxation of her thighs and the messages of eager anticipation relayed to her by her flesh.

They made her shiver urgently against him, a sharp moan of tension exploding in her throat as he kissed her breast and then slowly drew her nipple into his mouth, caressing it with his tongue and then, when she responded frantically to him, sucking on it until her back arched and her nails dug into the muscles of his back.

He kissed her midriff, counting the ribs, and then bit gently at the indentation of her waist, his hands on her hips and then sliding gently beneath her, lifting her, holding her, so that when she felt his mouth moving slowly against her inner thigh it was impossible for her to move, to free herself from the power of his slow and erotic intimacy with her.

She could not live through so much pleasure, no one could. Her mind went dizzy, her thoughts colliding as her senses took over.

She heard herself protesting, pleading that she be allowed the same intimacy with him that he had with her. And she heard him shushing her, telling her that that moment would come, but suddenly that comfort was not enough, just as the delicate tender stroke of his tongue was not enough either.

She wanted more. She wanted *him*; she wanted the fierce pulse of his body deep within her own; she wanted the knowledge that his desire for her was equally strong as hers for him.

Somewhere in the distance Charlotte could hear a noise. She moved feverishly against Daniel, wanting to blot it out, but already he was moving, leaving her, groaning reluctantly, moving slowly, it was true, but he was still doing it, deserting her for that imperative, intrusive ring of his telephone.

Achingly resentful of the interruption, she watched as he walked across the room and picked up the receiver.

'Patricia.'

Even without the name, Charlotte would have recognised the sharp imperious tones of the other woman on the other end of the line.

'I need to see you, darling,' she heard her saying. 'Now...'

Charlotte felt Daniel turn towards her and immediately, bitterly she shielded her face from him, sickness churning her stomach, destroying all her pleasure, stripping what had happened between them of all the emotion in which she had cloaked it and leaving only the stark reality that she had been on the point of giving herself wholly and completely to a man to whom she was simply an available woman with whom to have sex. There was no point in trying to deny the truth to herself, in trying to pretend otherwise. The other woman, the *important* woman in his life was at the other end of the telephone...a telephone whose ring he could have denied.

She was struggling into her clothes, her fingers numb and awkward as she buttoned her blouse. Behind her she could hear Daniel talking, his voice low and clipped, and then she heard the receiver being replaced.

She tensed as she felt his hands on her shoulders, wanting to shrug him off, to reject him as he had rejected her.

'Charlotte, I'm so sorry about this, but...'

Up until then she hadn't realised how much she had been pinning her hopes on hearing him tell her that the phone call was unimportant, that nothing mattered more to him than being with her, than loving her.

There was a sour taste in her mouth, a heavy weight against her heart. She felt sick with savage self-contempt, her eyes burning with tears she knew she must not cry.

'It's all right,' she told him tightly. 'I do understand that *business* must come first.'

She underlined the word business, burning to look at him as she did so. His nakedness should have rendered him foolish, but somehow it didn't. All it did was to reinforce all that her grieving senses told her she had lost.

If he came to her now, denied Patricia's claims on him, whatever they were—but he didn't.

'Charlotte, I have to go. It's a business matter. I can't——'

'There's no need to explain,' she told him tightly.

A business matter. Did he think she was a complete fool? Did he think she hadn't heard that low-voiced 'darling'? That she hadn't heard the office gossip? Or wasn't she supposed to mind that he was going straight from her to another woman?

The sickness inside her grew. She snatched up her jacket and her bag, her body trembling, unable to bear to look at him.

She reached the door, dragging it open before he could open it for her. She felt physically sick now at the thought of having him anywhere near her...sick with herself for her own stupidity, her own vulnerability.

When she thought of the things she had said, the things she had done...the things she had *wanted* to do...

Her whole body burned with the fires of self-loathing and despair.

She had reached the back door. Daniel was opening it for her, following her out to the car. Well-mannered to the last. She bit back the hysterical laughter tearing at her throat. Did he expect her to be equally well-mannered?

What *were* good manners in such a situation? To politely pretend that she was not aware of that betraying phone call, that husky 'darling'...to assure him that she quite understood?

She was way, way out of her league, she admitted painfully as she got into her car; way, way out of it.

She wasn't really in any fit state to drive, but she dared not stop until she was well clear of the area in case Daniel saw her on his way to Patricia Winters.

Would he spend the *night* with her? Would *she* be the one lying in his arms, waking up with him in the morning?

Charlotte cursed as her eyes were suddenly blinded by a hot rush of tears.

She'd thought she knew all there was to know about humiliation and despair, but she had never known emotions like these, never known what it was to confront the knowledge that she loved a man who, while exhibiting great warmth and tenderness, in actual fact felt nothing for her at all, other than an impersonal male sexual desire.

What had she thought she was doing? She had known before tonight what the situation was. She had known it and she had deliberately, wantonly ignored that knowledge.

She deserved what had happened to her, she told herself acidly, just as she had deserved the failure of her business. The fault, the blame lay at *her* door and no one else's.

She could have refused to have supper with Daniel, and she most certainly could have refused to make love with him.

She tried to envisage how she was going to cope in the morning, seeing him come into work, knowing he had probably come straight from Patricia Winters's bed, but her imagination simply could not grapple with what she was asking of it.

All she wanted to do was to crawl away somewhere and hide, to deny that she had ever known anyone called Daniel Jefferson, and certainly to deny that she had ever loved him.

If only she could be spared the humiliation of ever having to face him again.

She toyed briefly with the idea of simply never going back to the office, but she knew it was an option that just wasn't open to her.

For one thing, how would she explain her behaviour to her parents? Her face burned at the thought of even attempting such a task.

No, she would just have to find some way of brazening things out, of letting Daniel know that what had happened between them was as unim-

portant and meaningless to her as it obviously was
to him.

But how?

CHAPTER NINE

CHARLOTTE sat down at her desk. Getting herself in to work this morning had been one of the hardest things she had ever had to do, and that included facing up to the knowledge that her practice had been heading for bankruptcy.

Funny now how unimportant that seemed when compared with the intensity of what she was suffering now.

One look at her reflection in the cloakroom mirror before coming in to her office had confirmed what she already knew—that, despite the careful application of make-up, her face betrayed all the classic signs of immense strain, just as the puffiness around her eyes told of the tears she had cried in her sleep.

She was praying that at least for today Daniel would have the compassion and the sensitivity to stay away from her; he was compassionate enough where *others* were concerned, after all, and he must know surely how she felt.

She might not have said the actual words 'I love you' last night, but surely he must have seen...felt...known that to her what was happening between them was something very special.

But maybe he had simply chosen not to see any of that; to assume that because his interest in her was merely sexual so was hers in him.

Or maybe he hadn't even thought about her at all once she had gone and he was on his way to see Patricia Winters.

She heard his outer office door open, and froze, bending her head protectively over the papers on her desk, the words blurring in front of her eyes as she trembled inwardly.

Seconds and then minutes ticked by, and, although she strained to do so, she could not hear anything from Daniel's office, and the communicating door remained blessedly closed.

Work, any real constructive work, was of course impossible, but Charlotte ploughed on doggedly, reading the case file notes on the case on which she had been working, but she knew that her mind was not really concentrating on what she was supposed to be doing.

Every time she heard the slightest sound outside her office, she tensed, dreading Daniel's appearance.

At ten o'clock Anne appeared with the day's post.

'Goodness, you look pale,' she commented as she came in. She gave Charlotte a concerned look. 'You haven't got this tummy bug thing that's going round, have you?'

Charlotte shook her head. 'I don't think so.'

'I wonder what it is that Patricia Winters wanted to see Daniel about?' Anne continued chattily. 'Whatever it was, it must have been urgent for him to have had to call to see her on his way in to work. Unless it's just another ploy to get his attention— I can just see her, can't you? Floating downstairs in something black and sexy, claiming that she'd just woken up, but with her full war-paint on and her hair immaculate.'

Charlotte was shaking visibly. She felt her stomach start to heave as her body reacted to Anne's chatty comments.

'Are you sure you're all right?' Anne asked with some alarm when she saw what was happening to her.

Charlotte couldn't speak. She could only shake her head, closing her eyes tightly to force back the tears she could feel burning them as Anne fussed over her, telling her to keep still while she went to get her a glass of water.

It wasn't Anne's fault. She had no idea that she or rather her comments were responsible for her malaise. And yet why should she feel so distraught, so... so abandoned? She had known already that Daniel was going to Patricia Winters. She had heard the office gossip about the way Patricia had been pursuing Daniel. All right, so his staff loyally believed that *he* had no personal interest in Patricia and that she was the one trying to instigate a relationship between them, but Charlotte had been trained to observe facts, to assemble and to analyse them, and all the facts she had now made it perfectly clear that Daniel and Patricia were lovers.

Now all the mental images she had fought so hard to suppress came hurtling into her brain to torment her; images of Daniel and Patricia in bed together, images of Daniel as she herself had seen him last night. Images of him waking up to look at his sleeping lover and then reaching for the phone to lie about why his arrival would be delayed.

It was so simple for him to claim that he was visiting Patricia on business when in reality...

She swallowed painfully, telling herself ruthlessly, Go on, admit it... admit it... He went to her last night straight from your arms. He spent the night with her and even that wasn't enough, so that this morning he still wanted to be with her.

The pain that tore through her was harder than anything she had had to bear. It burned her skin and glittered from her eyes so that Anne, returning with a glass of water, took one look at her and exclaimed, 'You look dreadful! Are you sure you...?'

'I...I...have a slight headache, that's all,' Charlotte lied, and then, when she had finally persuaded Anne that she was beginning to feel a lot better, she wondered why on earth she had not simply accepted the excuse Anne had been giving her and gone home on the pretext of having picked up this bug that was apparently going round.

It wasn't too late, she told herself dizzily. She could get up from her desk now and leave. Anne would confirm her apparent illness to anyone who cared to enquire.

Perhaps a few days at home, to pull herself together, to get her life back under control.

She was starting to stand up, pushing her chair back from her desk, when the communicating door opened and Daniel walked in.

'Charlotte, I need to talk with you.'

She knew immediately that it wasn't business he wished to discuss; she could tell that from the tone of his voice.

What was it he did want to tell her? she wondered bitterly. That last night had been a mistake, that he would be grateful if she simply pretended that it had never happened?

Well, two could play at that game.

She stood up, keeping her body turned away from his, and her head averted from him, focusing on her desk, curling her fingers into her palms as she fought to keep her voice unemotional and even.

'If it's about last night, I don't really think there's anything that needs to be said,' she told him.

'Charlotte——'

She ignored the curt demand in his voice and continued, 'I... We... we're both adults, Daniel. What happened between us last night was... Well, I have to be honest with you, even though... I'm afraid I let things get rather out of hand. As I told Richard when he originally interviewed me for this job, I was engaged. That engagement was broken by mutual consent a few months ago... I don't like having to admit this, but, well... let's just say that I've obviously been missing Bevan, my ex-fiancé... What happened last night had nothing to do with you personally... It was... it was simply sex.'

Charlotte herself winced as she delivered the lie, but she had to do it, for her pride's sake. She could not, would not allow Daniel to be the one to tell her that she had meant nothing to him.

She could feel the silence pressing in on her, suffocating her almost, and then Daniel spoke.

His voice grated against her nerves—already on edge—harsh and bitter as he demanded, 'Are you trying to tell me that you were *using* me as a substitute for your ex-fiancé; that when you touched me...kissed me...it was this Bevan you really wanted?'

Charlotte winced, praying that the anger in his voice wouldn't carry his words out into the corridor where they might be overheard.

Why was he reacting like this? He should be grateful to her for making it all so easy for him, but then, men were notorious where their sexual pride was concerned. No doubt he didn't like the idea that she had merely been using him, even though they both knew that he had been doing exactly the same thing with her.

Even so, something in his voice panicked her, stampeding her into reacting defensively. 'I suppose you believe that a woman shouldn't feel like that?' she demanded recklessly. 'That she should not admit to having a need for physical...contact...for sex?'

Inwardly Charlotte was horrified by what she was saying, but it was as though she could not stop the words from pouring out, as though someone else were in control of her.

'What I think,' Daniel told her evenly, 'is that *no one*, man or woman, should *ever* use another human being as a substitute for someone else, either emotionally or physically.'

And then he turned on his heel and walked away from her, opening the communicating door, walking through and then very firmly closing it.

Charlotte sat down. She was shaking violently. What had she said? She went alternately hot and then cold as the full enormity of her claims sank in.

Daniel had been furious with her...furious...but he had kept his temper under control, apart from those icy words of contempt he had delivered before leaving her. Words which meant nothing, she told herself. After all, how could they when they were the complete opposite of the way he himself had acted?

But even so...for her to have claimed that she had used him as a substitute for Bevan, and for him to have believed it...

She told herself that it was all for the best...that this way at least she still had her pride.

By lunchtime she actually did have the headache she had pretended to have earlier in the day.

She had heard Daniel moving around in his office for ten minutes or so after he had left her and then he had apparently gone out.

She wasn't going to ask Anne where he was, of course, and she told herself firmly that she was glad that he wasn't in...that as far as she was concerned she wouldn't care if she never saw him again. In fact, she would prefer not to.

She worked through her lunch-hour, unable to face the thought of food and equally unable to face the sympathy of the rest of the staff when they saw her wan face. Besides, she had work to catch up on, but by half-past two, when she could barely see the typescript in front of her because of the agonising pain in her head, she admitted defeat, and rang through to Anne to tell her that she had decided to go home.

'I should think so,' Anne scolded her in a motherly way.

Mercifully when she got home the house was empty. She took two pain-killers, undressed, stripping off her suit and shirt, and lay down on her bed, but instead of the sleep she so desperately needed all she got were repeated tormenting mental images of Daniel. Daniel making love to her...Daniel making love to Patricia. Daniel looking at her with contempt and dislike...Daniel looking at Patricia Winters with love and desire. Daniel telling her that she was to work under his direct supervision...Daniel telling her about Lydia and John. Daniel...Daniel...Daniel...

She had just fallen into an exhausted sleep when her mother came upstairs, exclaiming anxiously, 'Charlotte, you're home early! What's wrong?'

Despite her mother's objections, Charlotte insisted on going back to work the next day.

She was not, she decided wearily, going to be accused of being a malingerer as well as everything else. However, once she did get to work Anne confirmed her mother's view by exclaiming, 'Are you sure you should be back? You still look dreadfully pale.'

Charlotte gave her a wry look. 'My mother was less tactful,' she told her. 'She simply said I looked dreadful, full stop.'

Anne laughed. 'I'll get you a cup of coffee if you like,' she offered, and then, 'Hang on a sec while I get the coffee.'

Puzzled, Charlotte waited for her to return.

When she did, she put Charlotte's coffee down on her desk for her, and Charlotte noticed that she had also brought her own tea.

'Well, you missed it all yesterday,' Anne began chattily. 'Of course, it's all supposed to be strictly confidential and low-key. For obvious reasons, Daniel doesn't want it getting out. I mean, it's all legal and everything now, but even so...'

Charlotte stared past her. Her heart was beating slowly and heavily, a presentiment of doom slowly numbing her.

'What is it? What's happened?' she asked Anne.

'Well, you know how I said I couldn't understand why Daniel was spending so much time with Patricia Winters, especially when her husband's estate had all been wound up? Well, I suppose we should have guessed, really. In a way it was obvious.'

She paused to drink her tea, while Charlotte's stomach churned sickly. She knew what she was going to hear, of course. Daniel and Patricia were engaged. That was the news Anne wanted to tell her...

'Of course, it is exactly the sort of thing Daniel would do... and I can understand why it had to be kept secret. I must say that I'm still surprised that he managed to pull it off, although the fact that Patricia Winters has got involved with this new man will have helped. He's very wealthy, by all accounts, and of course she'll want him to see her in a good light.' She grimaced slightly, her expression betraying what she thought.

Charlotte stared at her. She was suddenly totally confused. What on earth was Anne talking about? How could Patricia Winters be involved with a new man when she was engaged to Daniel?

'Anne,' she said slowly, 'I haven't a clue what you're trying to tell me. Are Daniel and Patricia engaged or not?'

'Engaged?' Anne stared at her. 'Of course not. No...'

'Then what...?'

'Well, you know that Patricia's husband was very badly injured in a car accident, and it was those injuries he died from in hospital, but before he died he sent for Daniel, and he told him that he wanted to change his will. Apparently he realised how unfair he was being to his stepson. He had quarrelled with him because Gordon didn't approve of his marriage to Patricia, and Gordon was forced to leave the business and the area because of it.

'Unfortunately Paul Winters died before he could sign his new will, and all these meetings Daniel has been having with Patricia have been because he's been trying to persuade her to hand over control of the business to Gordon, as Paul wished.

'Well, you know what she's like. At first she refused point-blank, but then she started hinting that she might change her mind. Daniel didn't say so, but I suspect that she's rather been dangling the carrot and playing Daniel along, using the excuse of pretending she wanted to see him on business when in reality... but then she met this other man, and the other evening Daniel had a telephone call from her saying that she was prepared to discuss legally signing over the business to Gordon, but that she wanted everything sorted out as quickly as possible because she and this new man are off to Florida for an unspecified period of time. He seems to have some kind of business out there—a share in a marina development or something.

'Daniel managed to get Patricia to legally sign over the business yesterday morning. That was the reason for his early call on her. Apparently they'd talked everything through the previous evening and then he'd gone home and typed up the papers himself. He didn't say so but I suspect he didn't want to risk leaving it too long in case she changed her mind.'

'I...I see...' Charlotte said faintly. 'I...I suppose Daniel must be feeling very relieved and pleased.'

'Well, you'd think so,' Anne agreed, 'but to be quite honest I rather got the impression yesterday that something was bothering him. Of course, it's John Balfour's funeral today—that's why he isn't in—and he was very fond of the old man.'

'Yes, yes... he was...' Charlotte agreed.

She was feeling sick with remorse and guilt, and, worse, she was agonisingly, bitterly aware of what she had done... of what she had destroyed...

But Daniel could have explained... He could have told her...

She bit her lip, acknowledging that in the end it all came down to the same thing—a lack of trust. He did not trust her as a colleague and she had not trusted him as a man. And perhaps after all what had happened was for the best, because without that mutual trust there could have been no real relationship between them.

Even so, she could not help reflecting on what her own misjudgement of the situation had cost her. If only she had not leapt to the wrong conclusions... if only she had waited, listened, accepted that when he had said it was business that he had been speaking the truth.

And most of all if only yesterday morning she had kept silent... not allowed her pride to push her into that disastrous outpouring of lies.

She shuddered as she remembered exactly what she had said to him, and then she remembered his response.

Daniel was back at work. He had responded to Charlotte's hesitant queries about John Balfour's funeral pleasantly and calmly but very briefly. Although the communicating door between their offices remained open, although he continued to walk through to stand beside her desk while he discussed various aspects of their work with her, although outwardly nothing had changed, inwardly everything had changed.

He no longer stood as close to her; she no longer looked up and found him watching her in that disturbing heart-jerking way he had done before.

Where there had been warmth there was now...nothing.

It was as though he had deliberately stepped back from her, distancing himself from her. There were now invisible barriers between them that made it impossible for her to even think of broaching the subject of the evening they had spent together and of trying to explain to him why she had reacted as she had.

She had made one attempt to open the subject by commenting on how pleased he must be at the outcome of his work on Gordon Johnson's behalf.

'It was not strictly within my role as a solicitor,' he had told her briefly. 'Certainly I myself was aware that in trying to carry out Paul's wishes I might be accused of trying to put illegal pressure on Patricia. After all, Paul's will as it stood was perfectly legal, but I knew what Paul's wishes were and certainly morally at least it seemed only fair that Gordon... But I'm a solicitor, not God, and it's always very, very dangerous to start believing that one has the right to dispense justice. I was extremely concerned that any involvement on my part must not in any way affect the practice; that was why the whole thing had to be kept confidential.

'I wasn't even able to discuss it with Richard. No doubt if I had he would have cautioned me, as I would have done him in similar circumstances, not to get involved.

'However, fortunately it's all turned out as Paul wished.'

He had given her a wry, almost grim look.

'Even so, it's not the sort of example I should be setting our juniors, and I suspect the Law Society would take an extremely dim view of it.'

'Yes,' Charlotte had agreed. 'And if Patricia... Mrs Winters had decided to lodge a complaint against you...'

'Exactly,' Daniel had agreed grimly. 'As I said, it wasn't the kind of situation it's advisable for any solicitor to get themselves into. Now, about this Hellier case...'

Recognising that he wished to change the subject, Charlotte had dutifully turned to the file he had been holding.

She had been so wrong about him, she had reflected miserably later.

Perhaps, after all, he had been right to doubt her professional capabilities.

In her dreams, over and over again she relived those all-important minutes when he had taken Patricia's phone call... only in her dreams she had known that when he had said it was business that he had spoken the truth. In her dreams she had held out her arms to him instead of rejecting him, had whispered to him that she would wait for him... that she wanted him... that she loved him.

But dreams were not reality, and by the end of the week she was forced to admit that she had destroyed whatever might have been developing between them.

Over the weekend she went to see her sister.

'What's wrong?' Sarah asked her gently as they prepared lunch.

Without sparing herself, Charlotte told her. 'I just don't know what to do,' she admitted finally.

Sarah's eyebrows rose. 'There is only one thing you can do now, isn't there?' she asked. 'You must go and see him. Explain everything, admit you were wrong—admit you lied about Bevan.'

'No. No, I couldn't possibly.' Charlotte stopped her. 'Besides, he doesn't want to know. He's been so cold towards me, Sarah.'

'Wouldn't you be, in his shoes?' Sarah demanded, and then she added more gently, 'Char, you love him, we both know that. All right, so he might reject you. He might tell you that he isn't interested any more, but surely it's worth at least trying to sort things out.

'Put yourself in his position. How would you feel if he'd said to you what you said to him? Of course he's going to be cold towards you.'

'But what if he refused to listen . . . what if——?'

'Char, *I'm* not telling you what to do,' Sarah pointed out. 'All I'm saying is that if it were me, well, I hope I wouldn't give up on my love so easily. Think about what's really holding you back. After all, what have you got to lose?'

'Only what's left of my pride,' Charlotte told her grimly, but as she drove home that afternoon she couldn't get Sarah's words out of her mind, and, when she came to the turning she should have taken for her parents' house, instead she found she was driving straight on, taking the route which would take her through the town and eventually out towards where Daniel lived.

CHAPTER TEN

AT THE bottom of the lane, Charlotte almost lost her courage and turned round, but then she reminded herself of what Sarah had said to her and of how much she loved Daniel.

Surely it was worth making this attempt to... To what, she asked herself in despair, to plead with him to love her in return? No, she couldn't do that. She didn't even know if he had *ever* felt anything for her other than mere male sexual desire.

What if he didn't want to listen to her explanations—what if he was actually relieved by the way things had turned out between them...? What if...?

It was too late to turn back; the house was in sight, and what was more she could actually see Daniel working in the front garden.

He had seen her too.

She watched him turn his head and focus on her car. He was frowning, his foot still on the fork he had been digging into the earth, and then as she brought the car to an unsteady halt on his drive he started walking towards her.

He was wearing a pair of old faded jeans tucked into wellington boots and a checked shirt with the sleeves rolled up, and there was a smear of earth across one cheekbone.

As she got slowly out of her car her heart was heavy with the weight of her love for him and with the hopelessness of her mission.

'Charlotte.'

There was no warmth in his voice, no smile in his eyes or curling his mouth, and the small tendrils of hope she had allowed to burgeon inside her slowly curled up and died.

It was only the fact that he was now standing between her and her car that prevented her from getting straight back in it and driving away.

It was useless, pointless. She had been a fool to come here and now all she wanted was to get away again as quickly as she could, but she knew she could not leave without at least saying something.

The words she had tried to rehearse all the way over here had deserted her, and with Daniel watching her in the way he was, so clinically and with such detachment, she panicked and blurted out, 'There's something I have to tell you.'

The look he gave her was extremely unkind. 'Really? Well, to judge from your expression, it isn't something I believe I shall want to hear.'

He was turning away from her. He wasn't going to allow her even to begin to explain, she realised, as, suddenly impelled by a surge of emotion she could not control, she ran towards him, catching hold of his arm, feeling his resistance to her in the tension of his muscles, but ignoring the message that tension was sending her, just as she ignored the hard set of his mouth when he turned to look at her.

'Please, Daniel,' she begged. 'I must speak to you. It . . . it's important.'

For a moment she thought he was going to tell her to leave, but then he seemed to change his mind, glancing from her to the darkening sky and then back again. 'In that case we'd better go inside,' he told her. 'It looks as if it's going to rain.'

It already was, huge heavy drops that quickly escalated into a heavy downpour as they walked towards the house.

By the time they were inside the sky was dark enough for Daniel to need to switch on the lights.

After he had ushered her inside he had paused to take off his boots. Some beads of rain clung to his forearm and Charlotte focused on them, her throat tight with pain and misery.

She shouldn't have come here. Daniel had already made that obvious. When was she going to learn to think before she acted? And there was no point in trying to blame Sarah—it had been her own decision.

'Will it save us both time if I say that I can guess what it is you've come to tell me?' she heard Daniel saying curtly.

The tone of his voice increased her misery. All emotion had been carefully blanked off from it, but nothing could quite entirely conceal his distaste.

How had he guessed? Had he known all along that she was lying about Bevan? She felt sick at the thought and at the thought of the fool she was making of herself.

'Daniel——' she begged huskily, but he overrode her, stating grittily,

'No, let me . . . You've come to tell me that your engagement is back on again and that——'

Charlotte was too stunned to lie.

'No . . . no . . . that isn't it at all,' she interrupted him. 'That could never happen. I never . . . Bevan and I, that's definitely over, I never loved——'

She stopped suddenly sharply aware of the emotion in her own voice, of the way it echoed with pain and distress. She was shivering, she discovered, but the kitchen was pleasantly warm.

'Charlotte,' Daniel warned her, and she could hear the strain in his voice and with it the thread of something else, something that told her that he was not going to allow her to back down now.

Suddenly she desperately wanted the whole thing to be over so that she could be free to walk away from him and from her own humiliation.

She lifted her head and stared at him, trying to ignore the treacherous pull of her own senses, the insidious ache inside that hurt her so much, the emotional and physical need for him she was fighting so hard to control.

'I lied to you, Daniel,' she told him grittily. 'When I said that I . . . that you . . . When I told you I was missing Bevan . . . I lied.'

She couldn't say any more. It was up to him now. Up to him to reject or accept what she had said, to invite her to explain.

And then, as she waited, he said the last thing she had expected to hear. 'I know,' he told her.

It totally destroyed her control. She headed for the door, half blinded by shocked tears, barely able to credit what she had heard.

He had *known* all along that she was lying. He had known she was lying when he had delivered that biting tirade against her.

He caught up with her just before she reached the door, leaning against it so that she couldn't open it, taking hold of her, ignoring the stiff resistance of her body.

'Charlotte, do you honestly think I believed for one moment that you were the kind of woman who would do something like that? Yes, at the time, in the heat of the moment of being rejected by you, I was too... too emotionally involved to listen to what my senses were telling me. What they *had* told me when I held you in my arms. You wanted me... didn't you? Didn't you?' he insisted.

There was no way she could lie.

'Yes,' she cried tormentedly. 'Yes, I wanted you. And will you please let me go?'

'No,' he told her unequivocally, and then he repeated in a much softer tone, 'No. I can't let you go. Not this time.'

And then he was kissing her, holding her, moulding her against his body so that she was left in no doubt about his need for her.

'Charlotte, Charlotte, I can understand your having second thoughts. I can see that I probably rushed you, panicked you, but why couldn't you just say so? Do you *know* what you've put me through, rejecting me like that?'

He was still kissing her, making it impossible for her to reply.

'Don't you ever do anything like that to me again,' he was saying to her. 'If you don't feel ready to make a commitment to me... If you want more time, if you feel I'm pressurising you, then say so. Don't, please, shut me out.'

He lifted his mouth from hers, framing her face with his hands.

'I love you,' he told her softly. 'I can't change that and I won't apologise for it. If you don't feel the same way about me then I shall have to accept it, but for God's sake don't lie to me. Don't try to tell me when I know damn well that it's not true that while *I* was loving you you were wanting someone else.'

Charlotte stared at him, her eyes brilliant with emotion. 'You love me.'

'From the first moment I saw you walking across the square. I didn't realise until I saw you going into our offices that you were the interviewee Richard was expecting.

'When Richard insisted that we needed some qualified help I didn't really agree with him, but he insisted, so I left all the arrangements to him, and then when I saw you...

'Perhaps I shouldn't admit to this,' he told her. 'It certainly wasn't very professional of me, and Richard I know must have been very suspicious of my change of heart when I told him that I'd decided that my work-load meant that I felt you should work exclusively for me as my assistant.'

'You wanted me as your assistant because...because...'

'Because I'd fallen in love with you,' Daniel supplied for her. 'Yes.'

'But I thought...'

She was glad that he was still holding her because otherwise she was very much afraid she would have had to sit down—her legs had suddenly gone alarmingly wobbly. Shock, she told herself...she was suffering from shock.

'Didn't you guess?' Daniel asked her, gently stroking her skin.

'I thought you didn't trust me. I thought you wanted to keep a check on me because...because you doubted my professional capabilities.'

Now she could see that she had surprised him.

He frowned as he looked at her. 'What on earth made you think that?'

'Well, you were so successful. Everywhere I turned I seemed to hear about you and your success with the Vitalle case, whereas I...well, I'd virtually only just escaped bankruptcy. I'd made all the mistakes there are...the classic ones. I felt such a failure, and then to have my work supervised...my competence doubted——'

She broke off, her throat thick with tears.

'You believed that,' Daniel was genuinely bewildered. 'But why...why didn't you say something?'

'Like what?' Charlotte challenged him. 'How could I accuse you of discriminating against me when I knew myself that you had every reason to do so? I so desperately wanted you to trust me, to respect me as a colleague.'

'But I did...I do... Charlotte, I saw your CV,' he reminded her. 'I *know* how hard you tried to get that business off the ground and I know how much

time, how much work you put in for which you
were never paid,' he told her gently.

'But I still failed,' Charlotte persisted. 'The humiliation of that, the loss of self-respect, of self-
worth—those are things you will never be able to
understand, Daniel. You've always been successful.'

'You think so?' He gave her a grim look. 'First
time round I failed my finals.'

He saw the look on her face and assured her,
'Oh, it's quite true. I thought I was invincible, you
see. I thought I knew it all. Lydia tried to warn me,
but what did she know? She was only a woman,
only a country solicitor. I was at university. In with
the "in crowd", as it were. Oh, I know what it's
like to taste failure, Charlotte, and not the kind of
failure you've experienced, the failure of genuinely
being a victim of circumstances. I was no victim
and I created my own circumstances. I wilfully ignored the warnings of my tutors and of the one
person whose judgement I ought to have respected
most.

'When I failed my finals I couldn't believe it. I'm
ashamed to say I wasn't even repentant, not at first.
It was everyone's fault but mine, and then Lydia
told me what a fool I was making of myself and
she told me as well how much she despised me, and
everyone else like me who wasted their gifts and
natural abilities, who expected all the good things
in life to be theirs for the taking. She told me outright that there was no place here in this practice
for someone like me. It was only then that I realised
how much I wanted to be here; how great a fool
I'd made of myself. I felt I'd forfeited any right I'd

ever earned to her respect, and I realised then how important that respect was to me.

'She told me before she died that she was glad that I'd had that experience because it had taught me humility. She said I'd be a far better solicitor for it, and, much more important, a far better man.

'Lydia had no very high opinion of the male sex, I'm afraid, perhaps with good reason. She was treated very badly when she first qualified and again when she first set up this practice, but those were obstacles she fought and overcame. They weren't without their price, however. I often wonder whether she ever wished she had chosen a different life, a life with a husband, children.' He kissed her gently and then said, 'Don't ever think again that I don't know what it means to taste failure, will you?'

Charlotte shook her head. She had been so wrong, and about so many, many things.

'The night I was here, the night Patricia Winters telephoned, I thought…I thought you were lovers,' she told him bleakly. 'That was why I said I wished you were Bevan.'

He gave her a long look and then said quietly, 'I couldn't discuss with anyone, not even with you, what I was trying to do. For one thing… Well, I wasn't sure even without my own conscience that it was entirely ethical. I knew what Paul's wishes were, but as a solicitor I also knew that his will as it stood was perfectly legal. I had no wish to involve the practice in the kind of unpleasant court case which could have developed if Patricia Winters had elected to charge me with trying to exert undue pressure on her, and yet at the same time I felt morally obliged to do what I could to see that Paul's wishes were put into effect. After all, he was an extremely wealthy man and there was money enough for them both. Not that Patricia was inclined to see it that way until Buzz Vickers came into her life. Hopefully he'll marry her and they'll make a permanent home for themselves in Florida—but you and I have something far more important to discuss than Patricia Winters.'

'We have.'

Charlotte gave him a mock-innocent look.

'Oh, I suppose you mean the Danvers's case. I was reading the file on Friday and I think——'

She stopped as Daniel picked her up and told her lovingly, 'Enough. What I have in mind for us has nothing to do with work.'

He was still holding her in his arms as he paused outside the sitting-room door to kiss her. 'You still haven't said it,' he whispered as he released her. 'Do you love me, Charlotte?'

'Yes,' she whispered back as she clung to him. 'Yes.'

'Enough to marry me? Enough to spend the rest of your life with me...enough to have my children?'

'Enough for all that and more to spare,' she assured him shakily.

He kissed her again and then asked against her mouth with a smile, 'Enough to stay with me now and make love with me?'

Charlotte laughed. 'Oh, definitely enough for that,' she told him fervently.

CHRISTMAS STALKINGS

All wrapped up in spine-tingling packages, here are three books guaranteed to chill your spine...and warm your hearts this holiday season!

#302 THE KID WHO STOLE CHRISTMAS
Linda Stevens

#303 I'LL BE HOME FOR CHRISTMAS
Dawn Stewardson

#304 BEARING GIFTS
Aimée Thurlo

This December, fill your stockings with the "Christmas Stalkings"—for the best in romantic suspense. Only from

HARLEQUIN®

INTRIGUE®

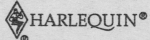